HUS THE HERETIC

BY
POGGIUS THE PAPIST

Published by
SHILOH PUBLICATIONS
226 Schellinger Road
Poland, Maine 04274
USA

Library of Congress Catalog Card Number: 97-65112

ISBN 0-9643914-3-0

HUS

the

Heretic

by

Poggius
the Papist

JOHN HUS

HUS THE HERETIC

BY
POGGIUS THE PAPIST

The first epistle of Poggius to Nikolai

I, Poggius, send you, my Leonhard Nikolai, many greetings!

As you will remember from my former epistle dated on Saint Clara's day 1414, I have been called upon to journey to Prague in Bohemia, to challenge the world-known arch-heretic John of Hussinecz, near Brachatitz, to appear before the Council of Constance, which will shortly convene there, so that he might answer to the fathers of the Church for his loose talk, teachings and preachings. I shall now let you know, my dear friend, what happened to me upon my pilgrimage and what mine eyes have beheld and examined here and there, because it is not given to everyone of our station that he may or must travel thus far; but do not expect fine words and style, only simple news and true arguments.

Travel I did, not on foot, but upon an ass, which I straddled on the fifteenth of June of the said year, after I had received the summons for Hus on the previous day from his Holiness Pope John XXIII, through Cardinal Goolvi. The morning was foggy, but soon the mist dispelled, and before I had ridden an hour from home, the sunlight continued to shine upon my road, to mine and the donkey's pleasure, since he had carried me, exceptionally tractable, as far as Gerstbach. There I only partook of milk and fish, as it happened to be fast day. While I ate, I remembered that I had forgotten the summons and left it behind in my prayer-cell, so that I was forced to ride back to fetch it. To the astonishment of my conventuals, I returned about midnight, seat-sore and devoid of all sprightliness. Two days of rest and a thimbleful of tallow healed my callouses, so that I felt fit to travel on, but this time I mounted more carefully and went the same way, which I had traveled before, as far as Lossenau and from there to the Abbey of Herrenalb where the pious brothers of the order of the Cistercensians took care of me lovingly. Two days I stayed in that paradise in the wilderness, then I proceeded to the hot springs in the valley of Wildbach. I had been under way for about the length of an hour when a terribly weaponed knight held the forest path with his charger, asking me whose protection I enjoyed?

"That of the blessed Virgin and her Son," was my submissive answer.

"Did not your donkey carry your body into the Abbey of Herrenalb yesterday, of which those of Eberstein have been the founders and protectors since immemorial times and still are, although these lazy busybodies in the cloister have renounced our protection and have asked for that of the Wuerttemberg prince?"

"I rode into the settlement to seek shelter for the night; I am a messenger and carry peace for everyone, I also carry a goodly part of ransom with me, to discharge any indebtedness, wherever I might incur it, for shelter and meals."

"Have you also ransomed your donkey's feed, watering, shelter and care with those of Herrenalb?" asked he of Eberstein.

"Not so!" I replied. "He found his feed in the fields until I rode on."

"Then your long-eared mount browsed in my territory, for that I ask of you five hundred hollow-pfennig feed money, for which I shall also give you free convoy to the springs of Wildbad."

"You cannot really mean that, my Lord! I do not carry such an amount with me."

"Then give me of your free will what you carry with you, you can much easier wander toward your goal unburdened and, by the way, I like your donkey better than you! Will you therefore come down from the animal's back?"

"Sir Knight!" I prayed, "leave me my carrier, for I am a punished wanderer upon the stony roads."

"That you should be; your teacher said so himself to your priors: "Go forth into the world, but not ride ye!" Thus jesting, he of Eberstein lifted or threw me to the ground, took from me my bag with the money it contained and went laughingly on his way with my donkey.

I had to drag myself, pitifully, on raw soles, to the walls of Hirsau. There I met the Bishop of Sulzbach who visited there. He took me in his carriage to Stuttgart and to Altenburg near Cannstadt. How different is that land from that in which we have our abode, dear Nikolai! Instead of the black forests, in which robbers and beasts lie in ambush, one sees vineyards and fruit gardens, and Stuttgart too, the court of the Wuerttembergs, is a pleasant township in which tile-roofed houses stand in orderly rows, beside the proudfully rising, well protected castle belonging to the feudal lords, said to contain a wine cellar that has no equal in all Germany.

Yet it is not alone the cellar, which is notable; wines too are said to be within it, such as no other court, no bishop's see from the Swiss Lake to Cologne, may boast of. Too, many lovely maidens wander about in Stuttgart, with rosy cheeks and yellow hair, of stately figure and not such half-grown ones as at home. The men have a martial bearing and I don't feel especially comfortable among them; to judge by their language, they are mostly adherents of the English heretic Wycliffe, they do not cross themselves and they mutter when they see the priestly garb. I would rather condemn the new teachings anywhere but in Stuttgart. The womenfolk walk about piously, chaste and without pouting, those of rank as well as the commoners. When night comes, the youths revel in the streets and make lovely music, using green leaves in their mouths, such as I have never heard anywhere and even in the morning they leave thusly for their hills and fields. They carry seed-grain and harvest upon their backs, the women upon their heads, which impresses me as incautious and stupid. The marketing is done upon an unpaved square, which is full of mire, away from the spring in its center, upon which a wooden lion sits, quite sternly to behold.

HUS THE HERETIC

They keep quite a lot of domestic animals at Stuttgart; every day the herders drive their cows, geese, goats and swine out to pastures, blowing upon long steer horns. At night, watchers walk about, calling the hour with strong voices, and singing rhymes. What one does need for nourishment and daily needs, is, all in all, unbelievably cheap, and I was told, that for an honest handshake one is often invited by strangers to drink wine as much as one wants, since wine is said to be more plentiful in Stuttgart than pure water, although I have not seen little of it. Water flows about the town, in broad moats of the castle, and at some places mills rattle, cast iron pipes shed water here and there.

To tell you, my dear Nikolai, more about the town, I'm not able just now, but if I am fortunate enough to come here again, I propose to see more and will make notes of it. I wandered away from there to Esslingen, Gmuend, Ellwangen, Aalen, Bopfingen, Noerdlingen, Waldmuenchen, Radpuza, Pilsen, always without danger and inconvenience, because from one stop to the other, if there happened to be no road, serfs of the cloisters carried me for hours upon their shoulders without a grudge. How different it became, however, the nearer I came to Prague, that nest of heretics. Ridiculed by the children, despised by the elders and spat upon by many, I could only travel towards Prague under cover, because everywhere Hussites were waiting in ambush to ascertain my mission.

The more lovingly I was sheltered by Arch-bishop Sbynko, who had ordered to be burned in his court more than two hundred writings of Wycliffe which were to be distributed by Hus. It was he who had forbidden Hus to preach in Bohemian in Bethlehem-Chapel. This heretic did not obey him, until after my summons, to appear at Constance before the council, had been brought to him. To this he gladly consented, more so, because the Emperor Sigismund had given him safe conduct, and protection had been promised him in my summons by our holy father, John XXIII, also Count Chlum, Stolzoh and Bokh had been given him as a guard by King Wenceslaus.

On the 8th of the Haymoon we left Prague and arrived, on the first day of the Autumn-month at Urach, a town in the lands of princes of Wuerttemberg, where a Count Eberhard had just arrived. This one invited Hus and his companions to travel with him to Stuttgart, so that he might show them honors there and festivities, since it was autumn now, which they accepted gladly. Six days prior to St. Gaul's day we arrived at said place early in the morning, and it looked as if the children of Israel had made their exodus to Canaan. Old and young were wandering into the fields to harvest the well grown grapes.

But when we came into the neighborhood of the city gate, down from a steep and dangerous mountain, many people stood about our coach, because they had not seen such wheelwright-craft before. And, instead of going into their hills, men, women and children turned about and followed us, to ascertain who was sitting in the coach. We stopped at the inn "Urban" for shelter and board. In the shortest time the house was surrounded with inquisitive questioners as to who had arrived, and when the curious mob had learned that the Bohemian Hus of Prague was passing through, there was unending whispering in all the streets of the town. It was everybody's desire to see the Wycliffian Hus, he who preached a new gospel without fear and ban. Many men came to the inn, to shake hands with us and to invite us to visit them in their houses. Among other excellent and well learned gentlemen there was also Albrecht Widenmeyer, called the Herrenberger, prior of Stuttgart, long a friend of the bishop of Constance, who had brought it about that the monks in his abbey were permitted to eat cheese, milk and eggs on fast days. Deep into the night there were discussions before open doors, quite civil and without hatred, about fundamental and less important matters of the church, entered by the prior, the clergy and some of the educated laymen. When I heard Hus talk, I remembered what the scriptures say: "And all of them became full of the holy ghost."

None were at a loss about what to say and yet every one's speech could be called proper, clever and excellent in every respect. Oh, dear Nikolai, how different now is the chamber of my heart!

Instead of the darkness of a dead belief, the light of understanding of the gospel has entered; instead of hatred and malice for the Wycliffian and other heretic folk, peace and forgiveness have embraced me in that evening hour and never shall I be the recording accuser about the deeds and neglect of my neighbor, as sure as the virgin, blessed from eternity to eternity, may help me. Already the day was dawning anew, when the assemblage parted with the promise, to invite Hus, after the holy mass on the coming noon, to exercise the preacher's office, for the running time of an hourglass and more.

Against the plan many of the young and older priests of the abbey, the monks and beggar monks protested, calling the plan a damned heretism, devils-pact and Babylonian whoring. The burghers though, did not bother much about the caterwauling on all corners and upon the pavement and none paid attention to the threats. Yes, one Peter Blanken and one Conrad Borrhusen, who the night before had heard the speeches of Hus at "Urban's," grabbed one of the cursing monks by his cloth, dragged him beneath the pump at a well and quickly pumped so much water upon him that his last hour seemed to have arrived. This would have really happened, had it not been for Fuenffer, one of the council, who happened by with two town-soldiers and safely saw the monk from the chaffing mob into the confines of the abbey. It is said that the same soup had been cooked for four or five of St. Leonard, because they had cursed everyone who came through the inner gate into the town to-day and condemned their body, soul, worldly possessions and eternal salvation. But those of St. Leonard were not satisfied with mud-slinging and cursing, they mounted the lifting gear at the gate and lowered the palisades, so that nobody could leave or enter.

This incited, as I have heard tell and have written down from hearsay, one Philipp Kessler, Dionys Zillenhard and Young Binkusser, so that they courageously stormed the gate, chased the hinderers away and lifted the palisades. Two of the men from St. Leonard were cast into the Giessuebel, near the bridge, by the angry burghers, the others were said to have escaped through the moat. No man, woman, child, hired man or servant girl remained inside of their four walls. Everybody, who had sound feet, hastened and scrambled toward the abbey church, not only to hear, but also to see, inquisitively, what wonders there might be, more so, because the majority did not know why they came there at all. For this reason the abbey people closed the portals to separate the curious mob, who filled the cramped streets and congested the narrow bridgelets. They lifted each other on arms and shoulders over the walls which encircled the church, so that the churchyard became filled more and more and a pressure was created from within and without. Suddenly, half a rod of wall toward the castle-market crumbled and broke down, killing several of the mob, others had their legs cut off by the stones and others again were slightly bruised.

When Count Eberhard heard of these events, he rose from his sick-bed and ordered the burghers to be quiet under penalty of corporeal punishment and disfavor, adjudged the abbey people, for their unthinking stubbornness, as being right, but not prudent and called Hus, with Count Chlum and his companions into his castle, where after a long discourse in argument and counter, the ostracized Bohemian priest was given a hearing, and was permitted to preach in the open courtyard before all the people according to his manner and belief. The fundamental text for his words he took from the Biblia Sacra, where, in the gospel according to St. Luke, it is said of the mild Samaritan: "Go and do thou likewise!" For a long time, dear brother Nikolai, I, thy Poggius, reasoned with myself, whether or not, I too, should walk over to the castle, to listen to the man summoned before the Council of Constance; finally I tired of worried reticence and walked across the few paces which separated the church from the county seat and came to stop across from the reformer, who stood, in all the black garb of the penitent, upon a stool, so that all eyes could see him and all ears could hear him. Loudly penetrated Hus' fiery words: "Love thy neighbor as thyself, and — God above everything else!" into every hearer's heart. More masterly, more courageously no apostles' holy lips could speak. There you should have heard, dear Nikolai, the interpretation of the parable of the proud

11

priest, the self-satisfied Levite, who had left the man, beaten and wounded, lying beside the road not cared for nor pitied by anybody, until a despised follower of another religion honored his own belief by the deed and not by hollow sham. And then you should have noted how he called the ways of our priests a godless idolatry, which is only a ringing bell and stupid salt, as long as hatred, pride, strife and persecution came from them and as long as they were not willing to heal everybody's wounds, be they in soul or body, manfully and without rancor. Yes, such teaching is not heresy, or Christ himself is such an heretic in every way.

After Hus had ended, Eberhard of Wuerttemberg offered him his hand and led him with his followers in his chambers and banqueted with them, for which he was censured by the gentleman of the Church, but was highly praised by the listening burghers. Following that was a festive day for Stuttgart; with sweet wine, jellied meat and white loaves everybody celebrated. We should have had to sit here more than a year, fat and idle, if we should have lent an ear to every welcome bidding or had accepted half of the invitations. For fully eight days we remained here, in which time we also saw unhappiness. First of all, four of those were buried, who had happened to be under the falling wall; instead of granting them an honest burial, such as would have been not more than right, the priests of the parish remonstrated, they closed the gate of the church cemetery to the biers, (to which act they were not entitled, according to my humble opinion) and did not permit the bodies to rest in sacred earth, those unfortunates, because, as was claimed, they found a deserved end in forcible acts against the church and had departed without confession and absolution.

For a long time the bereaved people cried and begged to allow their dead to be laid next to their brethren resting in the memory of Christ. They hoped for a granting of their request until the sun had almost set, but in vain! Thereupon great bereavement permeated the whole town of Stuttgart and my own heart seemed to burst for the woe of it; women came with their children and begged for clemency for their dead; all these found no attention. They came the men from the vineyards and many gentleman from the hills, who heard the request. Just as the wind rises all at once, there rose within the ever growing crowd a grim unrest. Within a few moments the entrance gate crashed and the biers were carried in to rest with the other honest bones. Even though the chaplain tried not to submit to force, courageously holding a crucifix against the crowd, he was nevertheless compelled to read the services since even Count Eberhard requested it.

The following day a strict order was issued that no one, be it who may, high or low, aristocrat or lowborn, young or old, was to speak of the dire happenings, as had occurred in the recent days, whether in the public houses nor in the inns, nor to tell first-hand or from hearsay to the young folks, under penalty of severe punishment and sentence. Further, Count Chlum and his companions were advised to leave Stuttgart and travel on to their destination. These honorable men had not to be told twice and proceeded at once with their journey and on the second day of November we reached Petershausen, situated opposite Constance, where I hastened at once to embrace you, dear Nikolai. But to my sorrow I was told that you had, due to the painful gout which has made you so cruelly suffer for a long time, left for the healing Wildbad near Hirsau, where I am sending you this epistle with the appendix, in order to intimately acquaint you with everything which might occur at the heresy court. That much I might dare to predict already, that all delegates, cardinals, arch-bishops and bishops will not be able to harm Hus, unless it be by force and unclean heart, which would be sinful and godless withal, which the Holy Trinity, whose protection I beseech for you and all mankind, may prevent.

Written on the third of November in the year of Christ 1414.

Poggius, Prior of St. Nicholas

HUS THE HERETIC

The second epistle of Poggius to Nikolai

Greetings to you, my Leonhard Nikolai at Wildbad! What I have promised you I shall attend to with this second epistle, to continue with my tale about Hus, where I have left off the last time. When the news came to Constance: "Hus, the arch-heretic has arrived!" there was a great tumult and no one's heart could await the day when Hus would walk openly through the streets of Constance to the Council. This then happened for the first time on the twenty fifth of November of this year, when he was called for a short questioning before several cardinals. He could hardly squeeze his long body through the masses of the populace, so crowded stood the curious, while some of them, here and there, squeezed his hand in deep concern, others encouragingly. Some felt urged to address questions to him about his new teachings, to which he answered fittingly, without conceit. But these happenings already lined up his preliminary judges against him, because they did not want him to be known and heard among the people, out of their own weakness. For this reason the Roman Legate and Mons. Zilliciri reprimanded him furiously, as if he were a demagogue and an evildoing renegade, full of malice and hypocrisy. Hus defended himself against that and said: "Where have I failed so badly and transgressed, that your Lordships admonish me so evilly?" Is it not duty so a blind brother asks in Christian mildness: where is the road? that I show him the road, as I see it? So that God will not punish me, too, with blindness, which I should have well deserved had I shown stubbornness. Therefore: Shall I not offer the hand to my brother, who offers me his in kindness and without malice and in peace to good deed? Would I not testify to vanity, pride, contempt, envy and other evil things by my reluctance, against which all Saints may guard us at all times! For we teachers and guardians shall be public examples in everything that is beautiful, just and righteous, as much as our sinfulness permits, since no man is able to make a pure sacrifice to God and we all are covered with leprosy and bad boils, which to acknowledge I am not ashamed upon this my pilgrimage. Then your Lordships demand of me that I should have kept silent on my journey here, but where man is silent, the dead stones cry out. For this reason I believe especially that it is well to open one's mouth when the talk turns to the lessons, to wisdom and to betterment and becomes no foul, idle gibbering, to the shame and dishonor of the Holy Spirit."

"We, the Chief Guardians of the holy Roman Catholic Church command you from now on, by the power of our regency, to quiet and silence and grant you only permission to answer modestly to our questions, without long circumscription and useless chatter. Have you heard it, John Hus, accursed arch-heretic from Bohemia?" loudly and angrily yelled Cardinal Goolvi, so that I, Poggius, standing in the ante-chamber, became suddenly frightened and wished inwardly for obedience and a good ending for him. But he, instead of obeying, raised his voice without fear once more and countered: "I am sorry for the zeal and rage of your Lordships, as I am the reason for it and beg your pardon for my manner of speech, if it seems somewhat outside of dutiful servility; but this you gentlemen might grant me, that I only talk, when my conscience urges me and that I always base my words upon the apostle Paul who forcefully says: one must obey God more than man! I was not called here to keep silent, it seems to me, and I have not left my homeland to be insulted at Constance, without respect for those who have sent me, but if I am convicted of uncivil acts, I shall gladly submit to a punishment, which would be due such a loose guest, but insofar as such deeds are unknown of me, I lift my eyes manfully before your Lordships."

Long the people waited for Hus to return from the cardinals; but the evening came and not he. Astonished and wondering the populace finally retired to their homes, strange worries seized his followers, joy and satisfaction his adversaries. On the following morning the rumor spread near and far that Hus, upon the demand of the Legate, had been cast into prison for unseeming behavior. Six weeks and several days passed without a word of Hus. Count Chlum and his companions remonstrated threateningly and full of anger about the incarceration and knocked on every door where they thought they might find help to free their charge, but in vain!

HUS THE HERETIC

Two of Hus' companions left for Bohemia to acquaint King Wenceslaus with the discomfort which had happened to their countryman at Constance. During these days, weeks and moons the arch-heretic was transferred into smaller prison quarters, well guarded against liberation. Often he was dragged forth from his hole, to be questioned as to his convictions, whether he had not relented and had changed them. Yet, just like the stone bastions which God's hand had built toweringly upon the shores of the sea, thus firm remained the Bohemian upon the structure of his opinions, which, according to his belief, bereft of all sandy foundation, towered above everything else.

And I, dear Nikolai, carry a like conviction within me, for Hus said: "What else is it, that you cardinals, bishops, and judges ask of me than to sin, by untruth and deceit, against the Holy Spirit? Do you know what happened, according to the testimony of the apostle to the man and woman, who denied their heritage? God punished them with sudden death, for they had thus blasphemed the Holy Spirit. And how much more would my soul deserve a terrible end, if I would bury the heritage that you and I have received, deny it and yet usure with it to the honor of God. You offer me gold and want thereby to hang a lock upon my lips; you want to give me rich revenues, clothe me in soft garments and give me well cooked food, so that I may be lost in everything that is called folly and worldly desire, leading to disaster and damnation. I tell you, that I will not finish in the flesh, like the wavering people of Galatha, what I have begun in spirit. Your law is a spoiled structure of sentences, just to no one, resembling stinking, foul water, from which truly no thirsty man can drink, in the midst of which all sorts of terrible beasts, worse than snakes, newts and salamanders, creep and wade about clumsily, at home in the slime, fearing the light and devouring all flesh which strays into their filth. And all this uncleanliness is to a great extent your, my present preachers, fault. For that, because I have the courage to shed light into this desert, you confine me behind dark walls, gruesome bars and iron-bound doors with heavy bars and locks, grant for my body less foul straw than to a murderer and killer. For the last three months and more I have not breathed clean air, as if I were carrion and already decomposing. And these misdeeds against me are committed by you, who have not as yet lent me a kind ear, who have not heard my evangelical teachings undistorted, neither from myself nor from others, only for the reason because you believe that it might bring you damage and dishonor, especially to your hypocritical subterfuge."

This sort of speeches I have listened to with my own ears. Oh, that I had to be the tool, to serve to persecute the man, who speaks thusly in truth without fear of any earthly power. Yes, dear Nikolai! if I lay my hand upon my heart's chamber and ask myself; for I had not thought that they would torture Hus, nor had I believed that woe would come unto him. When I recently visited him, because I had heard that he was suffering from an illness, I was terribly taken aback to find him in such a dungeon. Imagine the corner tower above the Rhine bridge, the waters flowing about its foundation. Ten spans above the water you'll see a small hole riveted thereto a grate of thick iron bars, through which, when the waves beat high, foam and drops splash into the dark chamber where Hus is sitting. It is necessary to descent thirty steps, the stairway being thrice protected by barred doors.

Finally one comes to a narrow chamber, which is as long and broad as a man is high, barely leaving in the light by the drafthole toward the lake, where the above mentioned splashes come from. I stood for a while in this chamber, before I discerned its outlines and then I saw the poor prisoner, who huddled at my feet in the foul straw. Upon a ledge stood a bowl with porridge, upon which lay a black, wooden spoon; next to it stood an earthen jar, near it lay a crust of bread. When the prisoner lies down, his head and his soles almost touch the walls. His clothing is falling to pieces and if he wants to relieve his bowels he must sit upon a round stonehole, from which a bestial stink rises, until the high water forces out the excrements from under the vault, which often happens only after three or four weeks.

HUS THE HERETIC

"Who approaches my prison, except you, guard? If it is a messenger of death, his visit be highly welcome, as I would like to enter the home of my Lord in peace!" said Hus in a hoarse voice when he saw two shadows before him.

"Poor John," I replied, "it is Poggius who is visiting you. To my great sorrow I have heard that you have fallen ill in prison, therefore it is proper for me to look after you, so that you will not harbor ill feelings for me because of my summoning you, whereby I have delivered you into bondage, which has brought you a great deal of suffering. At the same time I would like to ask you in your sorrow, if you have not become conscious of any false teachings or some other error, while thinking over your theories in this quiet solitude, since we all are human and are prone to make mistakes due to our vanity, pride, weakness or other unclean and ignorant qualities which we all are subject to from birth, and since no one need be ashamed of a change to genuine piety, nor may anyone be punished, be his belief what it may. Least of all your judges, just as the Lord, care to have you die, but they want that you desist from your hallucinations and that you will not persist in them and teach them, to the damnation of your soul and that of others, now and in eternity. Let us quietly talk about this, so that I may speak well about you to those under whose jurisdiction we stand according to divine and human laws."

While I spoke, the one I addressed rose slowly and leaned wearily upon my shoulder. "Your visit is worth much to me, for the sake of the kindness which brings you to me, honorable prior, because I have grown miserable in this dungeon, but I have never held the summons against you, which you have innocently brought to me and which I have followed guilelessly, sound in soul and body, only to waste away in the devilish claws of my enemies. Concerning my teachings and my words, my tongue has neither spoken a vain nor prideful word, nor any which I regret and I would never be ashamed to reconsider, in case I should find that I have erred or that my teachings were not rooted in the holy scriptures entirely. But I would like to beseech you to speak to my judges so that they might grant me a better housing than that which I am forced to inhabit, one, where I might look once more upon the blue arc of the sky before I die. And if it should be within your power and friendship to attain for me a public defense before the assembled gentlemen, for the sake of God, let me humbly beg you to do so."

Woefully I took leave of Hus and immediately hurried to Dominico, the Cardinal Legate. But this one's mind was strongly set against the prisoner and he was glad to know him in that stinking hole, for which reason I left him and went to the Chief Marshal of the town of Constance to ask him, for the sake of the five wounds of Christ, to provide better quarters for the sick man. This man arose immediately, after hearing my supplication, from his easy chair, grasped the baton of his office and said. "No misdeed against a deserted stranger shall find support under my administration, as true as my name is Stuessi. A just victor honors even a defeated enemy."

After a short while Hus was led out of his dungeon into a decent chamber, but his feet almost refused to carry him, he swayed as he walked; listless and unused to the day was the light of his eyes, deathly pale his cheeks and loose what was left of his teeth, since eleven had fallen out due to the damp prison. The nails on his fingers were terribly long, because he had been unable to bite them off for many weeks; upon his skin was a crust of dirt which exuded an awful stench and his otherwise brown hair fell in white ringlets upon his rotting and torn garb. His shoes had rotted upon his feet and his shirt and loincloth had vanished. The rounded flesh which had covered his bones had shrunken and shriveled and he had become a picture of woe without equal, unrecognizable to those who had known him before. Horror filled those who looked upon him and pitying people prepared a bath for him, brought shirts and clothing and refreshed him with strengthening foods, for which he could only thank with tearful eyes.

Thus passed three days in June of this year (1415), during which the fathers of the long heralded council were all assembled and the fifth day of June had been set as the first day of the general session, which decision had been announced at once to Hus, so that he might be prepared to answer to the charges which had been brought against him. Hus asked for a Bible to read from it the proof for his theories during the interrogations, but his request was not granted, nor was he allowed lead nor parchment to prepare his speech of reply; so he said: "What harm? I tell you, that, even if you would burn and exterminate the holy scriptures, I could replace them by heart, with the exception of the Chronicles. Therefore I am satisfied with my reason, for even if my body has been robbed of its vigor by incarceration, my spirit has retained its youthful wings, with the help of which I shall soar above the dust heaps and threatening animals with their sharp teeth and tongues yearning for blood."

And the day came on which the first hearing before the fathers was to take place. Not a stone was visible on the road from the prison to the church where the hearing was held, since the inquisitive mob covered every space; the houses were provided with scaffolding and ladders, because more than forty thousand people had collected with and without hatred for the arch-heretic. Thrice the bells tolled to announce the importance of the day and work ceased everywhere. The Cardinal Legate caused trumpets to be sounded from his abode and had the purpose of to-day's synod of the fathers announced and that every Christian believer, upon bent knees, should piously beseech heaven to grant a triumph of the Church over the portals of hell. Michael de Causis rode about upon a snow-white horse and denounced Hus with unchristian words, so that the hearers grew goose-fleshy and their hair stood on end. Such spite and hatred filled the hearts of the fathers.

When the clock struck eight, Hus rose in his prison and walked to the church as erect as his strength permitted, scantily garbed, accompanied by Wenceslaus of Duba and the Count Chlum, followed by the warden. At the church they found fifty-six clerical gentleman, two procurators and several scribes, seated at special tables, also eleven witnesses, who, soon after Hus' arrival, were sworn to the truth of their testimony. It so happened, while the oaths were taken, that one of the witnesses relented, because his conscience tortured him. He declared publicly that he had permitted himself to be bribed to give false testimony for a sum of money which he had been in need of. Quickly the repentant witness was ordered away with the death sentence: "Hang a stone about the neck of the perjurer and cast him into the water outside of the town where it is deepest!" And soon the bidding of the fathers was obeyed, the unfortunate man was dragged upon the bridge and cast over the railing so that he drowned.

After that, peace reigned at the church assembly as if no human life had been taken, although the executors of the terrible sentence called loudly and proudly through the portals: "The beast of an heretic has already gone to hell, into the Rhine!" After that Hus was clothed with a priestly garb by which act it was indicated to him that only in this garb he was being adjudged worthy of being addressed. Then he had to stand upon a newly fashioned platform which had been erected in the middle of the nave. First, the persecuted priest wanted to make complaints against his enemies, who had incarcerated him for eight moons, in spite of an Imperial safe conduct, Royal promise of freedom and Bohemian-Moravian aristocratic convoy; but the fathers, as well as the Cardinal Legate, forbade him, by the power of their office, every complaint and demanded only an answer of yes or no to the questions which the council had found to be in order.

Hus listened attentively to them, answered twenty-nine in the negative and one he answered firmly and with well-worded oration in the positive. Among the reported questions, however, were such of inconsequent accusations, which the accused refuted with calm collection and manly strength, but to the doubtful witnesses from many lands was given more credence than to the prisoner from Bohemia. A great tumult arose among the fathers through the report that Hus, after he had left Prague on account of the ban, was to have said to Cardinal de Columna, who had ordered him to come to Rome: "What sort of obedience is that to be, that I, as an unknown, wrongfully accused person, should travel three hundred miles, through so many adversaries, to my enemies who are to be judges, witnesses and everything else at the same time? Shall I permit myself to be dragged down in the consistory, forget my belief in God, unlearn my patience and, if I could not pay a bribe, be adjudged guilty in the most righteous matter, yes, and what's more, to worship the Pope on my knees as a God and crawl to him on my knees? No, I'd rather give the Roman upon the chair of Petrus a box on the ears, so that he would remember it for a hundred years." **Item**: "Pope John is a shameful beast and the actual anti-Christ, because he has started an unjust war, for the sake of his desires, against King Ladislaus of Naples; he permits indulgences to be sold to murderers, thieves, perjurers and all those who help him with their possessions, blood, money or hired soldiers." **Item**: "No solace is John for erring children, but a shameful murderer, because upon his command, the rascally archbishop Sbynko at Prague had caused the bloody death of three men there, for which God immediately punished Sbynko, by having a wild pig slit him open in such a manner that his guts were hanging out and none remained within his fat belly, and this just at the moment when he, as prosecutors of heretics, was on the way to see the Emperor Sigismund in my case and that of the preacher Jacobus Misnensis."

These and other accusations Hus did not deny at all, but he tried to prove what he really had said at all times. But now he was being loudly denounced, cursed and condemned in many tongues, so that he could not talk any longer and remained silent when Michael de Causis, in raving excitement, jumped before him and called threateningly with uplifted fists: "Now we have you in our power, from which you shall not escape until you have paid with your last farthing! And burnt you shall be, even if your thin bones have cost us so much money." He, who was thus silenced, had to take off his priestly garb again, after which they made fun of him, calling him derisively "goose-head," since "goose" is supposed to mean "hus" in the Bohemian tongue, and he was led away to his small chamber. The aged chamberlain Erlo followed him sadly.

"Friend," said Erlo to Hus, when they were alone, "you see, that I am old and my days are numbered, already I am eighty-one years of age. So listen to me and take to heart what I have to offer you in this lonely hour. As much as I have been told with assurance, your enemies have sworn death for you, be it by poison, should you be freed by the Emperor who is to arrive here to-morrow, or by fire if you will be found guilty; for this reason I shall show you the mountain from where help might come to you. Tonight, when the clock strikes one, be awake and prepare yourself for an escape. Under your bed you will find Austrian soldier's clothes, don them and hang over your shoulder the leather pouch which you will find, in which there is a letter, worded as if Vienna were its destination. Near the tree-lined road by the city wall, to which I shall securely guide you, there will be a swift mule, belonging to Bishop Wollra of Prague, who is for your cause, and upon which mule you may trot away with Emizka, the Moravian noble, whom you know, and who is a brave fighter and carries gold in considerable quantity. You can feel safe with him till you are with your King who has written to the fathers: "They shall not hurt his "goose," by his dire revenge, for she is to lay golden eggs for him yet." Be careful and without scruples!"

"What would happen to you, old Erlo, if you would be accused of having helped me to escape?" asked Hus cautiously.

"Let me take care of that. What would it amount to, if they should kill me in your stead, I would be of no use to anyone, I am almost a burden to myself and will have to pay the grave-digger soon at any rate. But you are not even or hardly forty years old and you can be of service to mankind in every respect. Now go to sleep, so that you may gain strength for your undertaking."

Thus the chamberlain Erlo is said to have acted, as I have been told by Hus in secrecy under oath and promise of silence, which I expect from you also, dear Nikolai. Further this happened: In the said hour of the night, Erlo went to the prisoner and encouraged him to escape, because everything was in readiness.

But Hus said: "Far be it from me that I should endanger your gray head by my flight, honest Erlo! Behold, I shall walk the path which the finger of the Lord has shown me. I would count it as a dire sin, if I should go away like a thief in the night and grant my enemies a triumph at the expense of my dishonor. No, I can't let this happen to me! What can human beings do to me if God's arm protects me? And if he does not protect me, the vengeance of my enemies would seek me out, if I should flee to the remotest ocean! At my ordination I have been bound by a solemn oath, to speak the truth without regard of my person: No one shall hinder me to do this duty, nor shall I flee it cowardly and become a traitor upon myself and my doctrines, so help me God! What good is a soldier if he runs away when his opponent approaches and what reward deserves the watchman if he sleeps with the others?"

"Oh, oh! that enlightening may come to you! escape! flee! as long as there is time, as long as the door is open and your friends await you. Your flight cannot be termed cowardly, but just, because your judges sin against you in disgraceful use of power and deny you justice and defense! Come, come! Flee, escape, before the cock crows!" urged the old chamberlain.

"Desist from your urging, your zeal and your request to me; just as the corner stone has not been set into the corner of the house to serve as ornament but to strengthen it, so unwilling am I to give way before malice out of sheer self-preservation. There is nothing which the Lord loves more in his people than that they help their brethren without thanks and offerings."

"You are a dead man ere the sun has gone down three times! Up, up! gird your loins and follow me! We have only a few moments, when those are past no one will unravel the net which is being woven about you. Come, come! why are you hesitating? Can't you hear that the watchman is announcing half past two o'clock and can't you see that this torch has almost burned out? Come, come! I beseech you, for the sake of Jesus Christ and with hot tears! Flee with me out of your dungeon into which malice has cast you!" cried and begged the old man of the hesitating one, clinging to him and trying, as much as he could, to drag him away.

Hus really went with his liberator as far as the outside of his prison, then he stopped and looked for a while to the sky, as if he wanted to ask: All-knowing One, is it not a sin before the Holy Spirit, that I leave the path which Thou hast laid down for me? And he turned, offered his hand to Erlo and said with a sigh: "Devoted father, I cannot flee! Let me thank you ardently for your work of love, and pray for me, should I go to my death. Convey to my friends my sincere thanks for their offer and ask them not to condemn me for my stubbornness. I shall trust in God and await my time!" Out of liberty Hus returned confidently into his narrow prison. The chamberlain sought out the waiting companion to announce his failure. This one was so furious with the old man, whom he believed to be a liar and a traitor, that he stabbed him with his dagger so that he fell. In the meantime Hus sang the Ambrosian Hymn in Latin so beautifully and loudly, that some of his enemies heard it and intervened for him, as a really pious man, wherever they could.

On the following morning, the sixth of June, two other strangers came to Constance: one of them with great pomp, the other without any show of splendor. The first one was Emperor Sigismund; quite a stately gentleman, with red hair and beard. What a crowd there was, dear Nikolai, as if the earth had opened up to spew out people to glorify, in a hundred fashions and thousand colors, the Imperial train. Singers, dancers and cither players, jugglers, jewelers, fine cooks and harlots had collected from every foreign land, to make a righteous or shady living here.

Alas, I thought, this is to be a council where abuses are to be done away with! Poor Bohemian! Under the howling of the people and the sound of your enemies' goblets ringing against one another, you will end as an exhibit for the blinded rabble. And as I imagined it, so it happened. Racing, fencing, games of all sorts filled the day and far into the night there was a noise in the streets as if the falls of the Rhine were outside the gates. Many-colored lanterns burned as far as the eye could see and young and old walked about in their best clothes, to eye the smirking Jews, the dancing Hungarians or the drinking bouts of the people from the lands on the Main and to listen to their raucous songs. Many tongues were heard and the garbs of many people were seen here. From Spain, France, Old England, Holland, Denmark, Pommerania, Prussia, Poland, Saxonia, Bohemia, Austria, Bavaria and many free towns of the Empire deputies had arrived and hundreds streamed in every hour, on foot, on horseback or in vehicles, through the gates of Constance to rest, wearily, upon the earth or on hot stones, because the sun burned like glowing fire from a cloudless sky.

The Emperor rode a supple horse which had white eyes, a fox-colored tail and a red mane. The animal's body was covered with scarlet cloth; silver pendants hung from it in silken tassels which were fastened by golden pins. On his head the horse wore a large plume and on his chest a coat of arms woven in colors, representing a double-eagle. The bridle was braided from pretty ringlets, adorned with beautiful shells from the depths of the sea. The Emperor was pompous in a black velvet jacket, blue silk underlined the slits in his trousers and at his knee started white, silken stockings which reached down to his red lace-boots. A narrow, long sword was his only weapon. About the neck he wore a golden chain, which was neatly arranged in diagonal loops, held upon his shoulders by hooks and which ended, under his heart, in a large, pearl-studded brooch. A white beret, lined with blue silk, covered his head; above rested a crownlet, the size of a fist, topped by a white, waving plume. Ahead of him rode a lean, sleek person, known as herald, who had to clear the road for his master. The Emperor's following was garbed as for a carnival, among them kettle-drummers and trumpeters, as well as several blacks from Asia.

The second stranger, of whom I spoke, was Jerome of Prague, whose clan call themselves those of Faulfisch, his rank that of a master of the free arts, professor and bachelor of theology. He is also a knight of the Bohemian King Wenceslaus and a devoted pupil and follower of Hus. He had studied at Prague, Paris, Cologne and Heidelberg. This man, like whom there is hardly another in learning and eloquence, came to Constance, to defend his distressed friend, which mission he splendidly executed, but by doing so he brought about his own death and destruction, which to report I shall by no means omit, but do later on.

As soon as he had arrived, he looked up Hus, who is said to have called out as he saw him again: "God be praised, that my courage has not deserted me and my feet have not become those of a fugitive, for a strong hero of Judaea has come to my side!" They have written together, so I have heard, a masterly letter, which I have, however, never read nor heard, because the fathers had not accepted it and had disregarded it with disdainful shouting. Jerome's is a beautiful body, only his face is pale; his eyes are coal-black, as is his curly hair. His mouth, in conversation, is exceptionally friendly and his teeth, in white, even rows, are entirely visible. His words are easy to listen to, whether they are spoken in French, in Italian, in German or in Latin. A noble golden ring shines upon his forefinger and he wears the garb of a monk without belt or tonsure. Archbishops, bishops, prelates and priests, even Prince Ludewig, elector of the Palatinate, visited him at once, when they had heard that he had arrived, although he is stopping in a small chamber in Sandstreet, in a house called "Ahlschleif," above Murdererstreet.

A lot of accidents have happened during these days, particularly during the day on which the two personages, about whom I have written arrived here. Bruised, asphyxiated, with broken ribs and covered with wounds many hundreds have been brought in; because the crowding was such, that the walls of the houses were bent in and the wainscoting in several ground floor chambers burst open and fell out. A leather merchant wanted to erect a maypole upon the roof of the guild house, misstepped and fell, the pole with the colored ribbons in his hand, upon the heads of the guffawing rabble, who stood below and could not move. But nobody was hurt and the man who had plunged down walked away, followed by the derisive remarks of those upon whom he had landed.

The dawn of the 7th of June 1415 came to Constance during such festivities and happenings, and, with it, the people were curiously about again. With the clock striking eight and the bells tolling, the procession of bishops, cardinals, fathers and deputies moved toward the church, where a chair had been placed for Hus, about which the seats of the gentlemen had been arranged. In front, toward the choir, there had been erected a seat upon a platform, covered with violet-colored cloth, appearing very costly. Above it was a sound-cover, from which hung, in long folds, a roof for the throne, which was decorated with golden knobs, pins, tassels and fringes. The gentlemen of the Church were clothed with all the insignia and the garb of their station. Many rode upon horses, donkeys and others were carried in chairs, such, for instance, as the arch-bishop of Sulzbeachen, a mighty gentleman, whom Ludewig, electoral prince of the Palatinate followed, carrying his train, not because of his duty to do so, but out of love for the arch-bishop who had been his teacher.

When all the front seats were filled, many more were admitted into the church, such who cared to listen, and there were not few. Thus Hus was brought in, clad again in priestly garb, in which he was led to a stool, which stood in the middle of the church and upon which the chair had been fastened, but without a back, as a sign that an accused rested upon it. After a while a regally dressed trumpeter sounded a call under the portal of the church and the emperor, with many nobles, clad in costly robes, entered proudly. Everybody took to their seats, also Sigismund. After that the chronicler rose, read the enumerated charges, of which there were forty-seven, to Hus, and of these he emphasized six serious articles which were:

1. The accused does not believe in the transsubstantiation;

2. despises the belief in the infallibility of the Pope and the worship of Saints;

3. disputes the power of absolution by a (vicious) priest and confession to him;

4. rejects the absolute obedience to worldly superiors;

5. rejects the prohibition of marriage for priests;

6. calls the indulgence a simony, sinning against the Holy Spirit.

For these and many other godless reasons and talks, John Hus is accused of arch-heresy and is called before the Emperor and the fathers of the Church to retract his teachings.

After that Hus raised his voice in such a manner that one could not have found the smallest corner in the wide expanse where he could not have been heard and well understood. "I have," said Hus, "awaited this day with longing and eagerness, on which, after long incarceration it was to be my lot to fight against the false, who have borne witness against me, and to talk about my doctrines, just as I have done in my homeland, without fear and timidity." After Hus had thus started, he was forbidden to continue and he was told that he was only permitted to make answer, concerning that which had been read to him, mainly, however, it was expected that he would renounce his error and turn from it in future and at all times.

"**First** of all," now spoke the Bohemian, "I am primarily accused that I do not believe in the transsubstantiation, and rightly so, because I cannot understand it at all. Because it is hardly to be taken for granted, that a little piece of dough, mixed from flour and water, dried in the sunlight, might change into a divine body, through which holy blood flows, or that it might be made, by the consecration of a priest, believing that the body and the blood of Christ are present in reality and are being taken, into a forgiveness of all of our shortcomings. This doctrine seems repulsive to me and nothing else can be meant by it but a symbol and as such is understood by many as "this is my body and this is my blood" especially since this meaning has been praised by many fathers of the Church and has been accepted by them as well sounding and proper, for the last six hundred years, before the Primate at Rome made believe that he can do thus and with him all those who have come out of his school.

Neither at the council at Jerusalem, nor at that of Nicea had there been talk about the actual transsubstantiation of the host, only about its use, instead of the unleavened bread. And just as nobody can really create blood out of water and wine, so nobody can create flesh out of a dough from flour; such a presumption on the part of the priests is sinful, ungodly and to be condemned; nowhere in the holy scriptures is there a foundation for it. As long as I cannot be shown, out of the Holy Bible, that I am in error, I shall insist upon my argument. Because it is written: "And he took the bread, gave thanks, broke it and gave it to his disciples etc; after that he took the cup, gave thanks and passed it to his disciples with the admonition that all should drink etc." It seems clear, that the last supper of Jesus was given twice and not in a single form, which is proven by the evangelical scribes Matthew 26, Mark14, Luke 22 and Paulus to the Corinthians in the 11th chapter, 23rd and 24th verses. Whosoever knows differently shall give witness before this assemblage.

Secondly: "I am accused that I harbor no belief in the Pope and in his infallibility in matters of creed, also that I find little or no solace in the worship of the saints. I admit this, my doctrine, in every respect. Because how can a man, even if he is the Pope, be infallible, since his shortcomings are the same as those of other men, from their birth on, and to err is his and everybody's main sin. Is it not written in the holy scriptures: "Nobody is perfect, only God alone!" To be infallible means as much as to be perfect and never to err; but as we are all mortals, we are all prone to make errors and we must all admit it. It is, therefore, a visible and serious deception of all Christians, such prideful and conceited preaching, that anyone, born of woman, is equal to the Lord and infallible; no human being's acts are so perfect, that nothing which he has done today might not rue him tomorrow. Further, no one has been given the power, to sanctify any man, however pure and godly he has lived, a thing which the Popes, for several centuries have believed to be their right. It is written in the holy scriptures: "Nobody is holy, I alone am thy God!" and again: "Nobody may call himself a Saint, but God!" And were this not written in the scriptures, then every man might ask himself just how far removed he is from salvation, if not every day and every hour bad thoughts and inclinations would come from his heart and if he were able to always subdue evil. If he wants to be humble and not arrogant, he must lay his hand upon his heart and say: "I am a great sinner!"

As long as this truth is present, it is to be taught and to be believed, that there are no Saints before the Lord and that to worship them is of no earthly use, but is only empty babbling. God is a spirit and whosoever prays to him must call to him in spirit and in truth. How can I call to him in truth, if I must ask a third for his intervention? He is the father of us all and his heart is opened to everyone with the same love; he is not nearer to this man or farther removed from this one than from any of us, and before him we are and will remain earthen vessels, which are formed today and are broken tomorrow, vessels which cannot ask preference on account of their shape. This would figure out something like this: I have not courage enough to talk to the Father myself, so you, Saint Benameter, do it for me for all times. And finally, who will be the highest and lowest in heaven? Who knows that? Who has ever noticed such preference before others? As long, I repeat again, as we all are begotten from sinful seed, there may be righteous men, but no Saints.

Thus said Paulus to Timothy in the second epistle in the second chapter: "And if one strive in the games, he is not crowned if he hath not observed the rules." What does it mean, observe the rules? Perhaps much fasting, praying and chastising. But nobody should boast of it, said Paulus to the Ephesians in the second chapter. It is also written: "Wherein in times past ye walked in sin, ye are children of disobedience and have sinned."

Whosoever knows differently, bear witness before this assemblage.

Thirdly: My enemies accuse me that I do not honor the confession as a godly institution and despise the absolution by a (vicious) priest; this accusation is true and I cannot renounce it here. The Roman teachers of the church say, of course, that Christ had said: "Receive ye the Holy Ghost: whose soever sins ye forgive, they are forgiven unto them; whose soever sins ye retain, they are retained."

But how can, you ask, a priest, who is the true disciple of Christ, forgive sins and keep them, if he does not know them? To this I answer and teach: in that he leaves to every conscience the penalty and resolve for betterment, with a stern admonition to be pious and to renounce all evil, to shed sins and faults and to seek grace with God and man. Aside from this there is written in the holy scriptures: "Nobody may forgive sins, but God!" Who, out of his free will, wants to announce the sins of his soul, may be enriched by it, but who cannot do this, the fetters of hell shall not be ringed about him. Even Jesus has not declined to offer the cup of reconciliation to his traitor Judas during the last supper, but he left it to the others whether or not he had done right, although he was more than a high priest.

And what shall I say of the absolution by a (vicious) priest, such as are sitting by the hundreds in the confessional cells, with a heart steeped in iniquity and filled with rude and ignorant thoughts? Those who in the morning read the holy mass with lazy tongues and then gorge themselves, so that they have to throw up again the filth with disgusting convulsions in secret places. Those who leeringly sit at eventide behind their large goblets and stammer with heavy tongues their "*Ave Maria*" and after they have done so, immediately wet their fingertips on drooling lips so that they might better grip their cards, which had been laying idly before them for a moment. Those who sit in a heap of dung and have quarrels with all children of man, who curse and revel, just like soldiery in the enemy's camp. Those who play the fiddle and reed at kirmess time, as if they needed the dance offering and had not enough to live on and too little to die. Those who linger about in lighted and darkened corners, where a sleek, nicely buxom wench might be scrubbing, milking or working, to make conversation, to embrace them in an unsavory manner, to enjoy lustful sights, and, where ever possible, forgetting all honor, reputation, modesty, pledge and station, commit adultery, disregarding marriage vows, and betrothal of those they rape. Those who do not know, out of sheer laziness, how to pass the time of the day, to come to a hunt-meet, egg hunt, cockdance, St. John's fire or a young pig roast, or be dragged there, on the back of a horse, a donkey, upon a peasant or upon a buxom woman, if these are zealots of the monastery. Those who carry daggers within their habit, so that they, if the fist proves inadequate or duped and deceived husbands surprise them, might defend themselves in self-made law. Those who sit all too often in deeper darkness of mind than those who come to confession and who know less of God and his gospel than the unreasoning heathen, against whom they argue and cry damnation here and there! Those, whose hearts are harder than iron and stone and less conciliatory than the blood thirsty beasts of the forest, which to observe everybody has an opportunity, by witnessing the torture which becomes the lot of those who contradict them, censure them for their sins and never want to believe what they teach or preach.

It is almost a crying need for God to send again His son from Heaven, so that he should breathe into them once more of the Holy Spirit and enlighten them and lead them to knowledge of himself. Just as no blind man is able to show the road to another blind man, under the cited circumstances, so no priest is able to forgive sins, which he commits, more or less, himself. "Without me," says Christ, "ye cannot undertake anything!" and "I am the road and the truth and the life!" and "Whosoever wishes to be my apostle must also carry my cross." But where have priests seen through Christ's eyes, in whom they do not believe and whom they carry not in their hearts?

Their ways are not His and not the Truth, but their own bad thoughts and cunning show them the road upon which they smugly continue. They shy from bearing the cross and make other people carry their loads. They drop everything which seems burdensome to them, yea, were it given to them to stave off death, they would enlarge the pockets of their habits so that they might snatch into them still more gold, to live without worries and in eternal enjoyment. This I call to serve Baal and not Jehova. And since the priests are not born again, do not sit in purity of heart, simple and chaste in their confessional chairs, I shall continue to preach and make known, wherever I have opportunity, that anyone, so he confesses his sins before God, should turn from evil and seek salvation. Have I said too much, then punish me for lying, ye fathers assembled in council!"

This started grumbling and adverse talk among some of the Bishops and Elders, but the Emperor raised his right hand and waved it until there was silence and Hus continued to speak after he had taken a sip of water.

"**Fourthly**: I am being condemned and shunned, because I am unable to acknowledge absolute obedience to earthly authority. I admit this accusation also and am not at all willing to recant what I have taught about this point. Although I know that obedience is better than sacrifice, this sentence cannot be reasonably interpreted differently than: "Fear God and love thy neighbor; then thou shalt achieve more by obeying God's commandments than by offering up a sacrifice." But that human laws are to be obeyed unquestioned, is a senseless demand and humiliates man, who stands in high regard, below his station and god-given wisdom, while he gains nothing. Even the Christians of the earliest times argued against their superiors thusly: "One must obey God more than man!" I also so argue and ask of you Lords: Is it just that the Primates of Rome demand that their wishes are to be preferred to the welfare of many thousands in other lands? Is it just the Popes curse those who break away from the Church and excommunicate them and call those benefactors of the Church, who murder the condemned? Is it just that a priest may announce this curse from the pulpit in a house which is consecrated to the God of atonement, denying defense to the condemned, that he may, as servant of the Church, sharpen the dagger against his friend and mix poison for him who had begotten him? Is it just that the Princes of the Church order their subordinates to see that everybody, be it in days of health or such spent in sickness, but especially when on the deathbed, makes a last testament in favor of the church or of a monastery, disregarding even the poor orphans and then demand the teaching of this creed: 'The larger the gift, the shorter the stay in the grave!' and: "The more magnanimous the stipend, the better the position in heaven!' 'The richer the estate, the colder the fires of hell!'" Is it just to beguile young hearts for the sake of gold, as Rome has ordered, so that they leave, contrary to common sense and laws of nature, this free and beautiful world and, forgetting all obligations to relatives, brothers, sisters and parents and the happiness of their souls, enter a convent, wherein vows must be taken which have, so far, been rued by every heart and could not be kept?

Is it just that the Popes teach the creed and that the priests call it well done, that every present made to the Church, even stolen property, must be retained and cannot be returned to the one from which it had been stolen? Is it just that the priest receives a confession as a sacred and inviolate sacrament; but should something detrimental against the superiors be heard in the confession, the chambers of the sanctum must be opened? Is it just that we are to hound those of a different faith, more so, because our faith is one of education and not an inborn one and the Holy Ghost is spread over all people? I shall not further ask about this or yon demand, each man's conscience must and will tell him that the priest, if he obeys unquestioning his superior, will sin more than his flock. Is it just, that the priest must erect a maypole and bless it, after fanatics and heretic-hunters, sent from Rome, have crucified an individual here or there, have tortured him to death and burnt him in the place where the pole is to stand? Only for the reason that the clergy, from the papal purple to the habit of the serving brother, may not forgo even as much as a grain of dust and that Sin and Lust may go on unhindered? For this reason I know quite well, and have come to know with grief, that I would have been permitted to drive ten thousand Jews to death with diverse tortures rather, than say and preach, what I have said and preached, before all mankind; no hair upon my head would have been harmed because of such deeds, but since I do not care to live in papal darkness and refuse to obey that which is against my conscience, I am intrigued against as a monster, out of sheer ignorance and blind obedience. Who is to forbid me to speak thusly? Since I have taken an oath at my ordination to speak the truth to everybody, and 'everybody," includes, to my thinking, Pope and laymen, Emperor and soldier, I cannot keep silent because of fear, but I shall obey God, whom I have called upon as a witness and avenger when I was ordained, more than man. If I have sinned against my oath, then I demand from this assemblage, by the holy power of the command which brought me here, to show where my tongue has spoken falsely."

Fifthly: It is held against me that I teach and preach against the current simony and so called mess of indulgences. My adversity against it seems to me a truly apostolical-evangelical one and I don't censure and preach more energetically against anything than against such a sinful trade, more so, because nothing else appears more godless to me than to commercialize the forgiveness of sins, to deceive the poor and miserable people and keep them in the belief that heaven might be bought with a few farthings. And why is all this done? For the reason that the Primates at Rome might carouse in splendor. Six years ago Dionys Nauclerius reported, when he visited me in Prague and perceived an image of Jesus' sufferings upon my table, shortly thus: "Before I went to Rome, my heart was filled with pious adoration for this image and I also honored the vicar of Jesus as equally holy with the crucified man from Nazareth. But when mine eyes beheld the capital of the crosier, astonishment filled my foolish heart. Instead of the mild fatherly picture of the superior prince of the church,

I saw four men carry past me a youth swaddled in purple, gold and diamonds, who was supposed to be the vicar of Him, who did not possess enough upon which to lay his head. His face was impertinent, haughty, covered with the traces of passion; upon his head he wore a triple-tiered velvet cap. Heavy, golden crosses dangled from his earlaps, distorting them in an ugly manner. His fingers, from the thumb to the little one, were covered with glittering gold rings, and the fastening which held his cape at the throat resembled the seven-colored rainbow, sparkling with rubies, jaspers, topazes, sapphires, emeralds, opals and diamonds, recalling the holy of holies at Jerusalem, of which is written in the old testament. Upon his calves he wore azure silk stockings and his slippers were woven from golden thread, covered with golden buckles and points. In such splendor I also saw him ride to pleasure on the following day upon a white horse and several days later I saw him on the balcony of his palace, standing there in a like splendor, witnessing the decapitation of several heretics, whose nude bodies were then cast before some captured beasts of the desert.

They seemed much more merciful than Pope John, the twenty-third of his line, enjoying the blood of those unfortunates, because they did not tear them apart, but lapped up mercifully the cut-off heads and the bleeding torsos. At his side stood a young maiden, more beautiful than any I had ever beheld, with whom the Prince of the Church jested, while the unfortunates were being led to their death. Wherever the Primate is seen, the people sink upon their knees and crawl before him. But not alone the Pope exhibits such treasures, several other princes of the Church do likewise, such as are termed Cardinals, Legates, Arch-bishops, Bishops and Priors. Upon splendidly bedecked donkeys they ride about, from one orgy to another, always accompanied by handsome boys and exquisite maidens. This is a life, which no man can imagine to be more voluptuous. Alas, I sighed then, oh Saviour! Are these your disciples, whose feet you have washed as an indication of your modesty and lowliness? Where do these debauchers preach your faith? Where do they still ascend with you the mountain of olives? And where do they still pray with you: "Father, if possible, take this cup from me!" But instead of the cup of woe they drink the honey of lust, instead of making the pilgrimages to Golgotha to crucify their flesh, they walk upon the flowery meadow of sensual joys! Who then, seeing Rome, this den of sins, would be surprised to see God visit this city with a fiery rain as he did Sodom?"

Thus Nauclerius told me, John Hus. And I caused to have carved from lindenwood, an image of the crucified redeemer's vicar on earth, the Pope, as he had been described to me, took both images, carried them into the university's assembly room at Prague and attacked the indulgence by presenting to my pupils the truth and making known to all people what a terrible monster the Roman clergy really is and how they gobble up all the fruits of the people's labor by prostituting all the world, with their letter of indulgence, in a shameful and godless manner. How can such priests of Baal still convey the Holy Spirit by prayer or laying on of hands, as had been done in the times of the Apostles? Simons they are, like he, of whom is written in the eighth chapter of the Acts: "And when Simon saw that through the laying on of the apostles' hands the Holy Spirit was given, he offered them money saying, give me also this power, that on whomsoever I lay hands, he may receive the Holy Spirit! But Peter said unto him, thy money perish with thee, because thou hast thought that the gift of God may be purchased with money. Thou hast neither part nor lot in this matter: for thy heart is not right in the sight of God. Repent therefore of this thy wickedness, and pray the Lord if perhaps the thought of thy heart may be forgiven thee. For I perceive that thou art in the gall of bitterness, and in the bond of iniquity."

Sixthly: "I am to be severely remanded, because I have preached against celibacy, do not honor this church dogma as a sacrament and condemn it as unnatural. What I have said about it, I am courageous enough to repeat here as my common sense dictates. Primarily I ask: Why does the Roman Catholic church teach seven sacraments, of which no Catholic may rightfully partake? Is not a sacrament a power of salvation in this life and the life after death?

But whosoever becomes a priest, forfeits one sacrament, that of marriage and only six items of salvation remain for him. For this reason he, who is not a priest, also has but six items of salvation, because he has not been ordained. Is this not in itself a confusing and illogical dogma: to teach the existence of seven sacraments and grant but six to all people? Furthermore, many centuries have passed since the foundation of Christianity and bishops and priests have wedded and permitted themselves to be wed in honor and decency, until some Primates, Gregory VII (also called Hildebrand) and Innocent III, thousand years after the death of Jesus the Nazarene, conceived the thought to forbid marriage to priests, so that they would not love their families, would not honor their home and would be compelled to seek salvation under the wing of Rome only, remembering the protection which was to come from there against worldly powers.

And what shall I say about the unnatural trend of such a request? Has not God himself instituted marriage, as a means to satisfy the craving for love in all men, even in all animals? Is not he, who becomes a priest, also made of flesh and blood? Just as his heart is not unresponsive to nature, into which God has placed all creatures for enjoyment, and has given us reason, by which we are told to live wisely, so the priest cannot do justice to this most severe of all human commands. I still believe that celibacy brings greater temptation to this one and less to the other, but it is certainly true that none are able to fight the battle for chastity with saintly demeanor! A battle, in which upon one side giant Mother Nature and upon the other the binding oath are enemies. And does not Paul write to Timothy in the third chapter: "A bishop then must be blameless, the husband of one wife, discreet, sober, of good behavior, given to hospitality, apt in teachings, not given to wine, or to blows, but patient, not a brawler, not a lover of money, one that ruleth well his own house; having children in subjection with all gravity." Better it would be if he marries, not because of a law, but for the honor of God and Jesus Christ. For those are speaking lies in hypocrisy, who have a seared conscience, who forbid a life in marriage and abstain from foods which God has created. I hold this to be the seed of iniquity and the root of all evil, the fact that the priest does not marry. God forsakes him, because he has turned from God. He sinks into oblivion because neither a wife nor children bring happiness into his home, he seeks not salvation, but the tawdry atmosphere of bawdry houses, turns to feasts of eating and drinking and makes his own desires his God. He turns to the other sex, baits those who have husbands, lures those who are widows or those who are simple maidens. And if he does not do so, he abuses his own body, so that it withers, or he fornicates with known harlots, to the ridicule of his parish. Only those are children of God, who are filled with the spirit of God and not those who live in rebellion according to a man-made law!

Thus I preached, and my words were open for everybody's weighing and judging. Too many complaints have been made and the clergy is despised in too many places, for me not to call him a cheap hireling, who does not speak against celibacy and who does not utter the honest, well meaning wish, like the aged bishop Paphnitius of Nicaea: that our Church might not burden its priests with a heavier load than other men. Whosoever is capable of proving me wrong, may do so before this assemblage!"

The clerical Lords could not contain themselves any longer, they yelled in maniacal ire, disregarding the presence of the Emperor entirely, not hearing the voice of the chairman: "Hus, the Satan, is an heretic! and arch-heretic! worse than Ariel, such as none has come out of hell to this day. Cast him out into the darkness, to his lot of wailing and gnashing of teeth! so that he may pay all his dues and perish in the fire. Burn him, burn him, for he is a monster such as hell has never before cast out, to be despised by all Christians. Cursed be he who has begotten him, the mother who has brought him into the world, the breast which has suckled him, the hands which are cared for him and the arms which have carried him! Cursed be the teachers, who have educated him, the friends who have surrounded him and the ears which have heard him in pleasure. Cursed be the land which is his home and the air which he has breathed!"

"Stop, you godless maledictors!" thundered the Bohemian Count Chlum, who stood next to the chairman and waved his sword threateningly above his head. "Death to him," he cried, "who harms a hair upon the head of Hus, my charge! Are the Emperor's regard, dignity, power and letter of safety thusly honored by papists? How can you so rave against and curse one who is more just than all of you! Not with curses has Christ visited his adversaries, but with blessings! Are you so inflamed because he has shut your snoots for you, you Sadducees and Pharisees? Are you so enraged because he has lifted the wing of him who voluptuously sits upon the chair of Peter and has shown what sort of bird hides beneath the glittering feathers? Is it a crime that he shows in what sort of stinking slime the clergy feels at home now and has no felt for the past centuries, how you sit idly behind the walls of churches and monasteries, how you feast upon the fruits of the people's labor and how you falsify the teachings of Christ and interpret them to your advantage? Is it an overt act of Hus to open for you the sacred bible and admonish you that your teacher walked in modesty and not, like you, in pride, in silk and gold? He gave to Peter, his disciple, the key to open all hearts and the heaven of faith with it, but not the sword, to slay, as you slay all those who do not accept your worldly doctrines and who evade them. . ." "Be still, heretic! or our curse be upon you also and upon the entire Bohemian lands!" the maniacs raved and a weapon flashed in every fist.

"My Emperor!" called Count Guenther of the Palatinate, "how can you tolerate such sin before your eyes, have you received the sword so that it may remain sheathed against the blackcoats?"

"Trumpeter, blast the attack," cried the Archbishop of Mainz, "that all Christian believers might gather to protect the Holy Church against the Portals of Hell!"

Sigismund paled, trembled and stuttered like a prisoner, until the Elector Ludewig raised his voice, not exactly in dulcet tones: "In the name of the head of the Empire, my Cousin Sigismund, who sits here upon his throne, I command immediate quiet and silence, or every culprit shall suffer with his life and possessions as a disturber of the peace of the land!" Slowly and one after the other, the Lords sat down again, and peace entered once more the nave of the church, in which there was a stifling heat and such a dust that one could hardly see a person any longer. Then the chairman announced the end of the session and ordered the continuation of the council for the afternoon. Many were not satisfied with this, especially the papists from Italy. They demanded a vote, to determine what should be done with Hus and demanded to know what the Emperor thought of the arch-heretic's defense and speech. But Sigismund earnestly warned against force, urging or haste and docily promised an honest reply. Full of rancor the Lords left their seats and whispered to one another to keep an eye upon the Bohemian "goose" so that it would not fly away, leaving the council open to derision.

My heart beat furiously, dear Nikolai, when I rose from the noon meal, to go again within the gates, because I had a premonition of the Bohemian priest's fate. "Woe, thrice woe!" I called, with arms raised over my gray hairs. How gladly I would lose an eye, cut off a hand, or, if this should not be sufficient punishment, would I give my life, if I had not had part in Hus' coming here. You know best, dear friend, next to God, what my innermost self is like, and for this reason I will not omit to say, that everything, which Hus had said and to which he had manly and honestly testified, had been deeply engraved upon my soul and had been spoken out of my own heart, for which I regard him highly and love him. He did not place his light beneath a barrel, but has made it shine into the dark places of unbelief, into such where I also had sat, my eyes filled with the salt of ignorance. Not many, like myself had lived within the law and according to the rules without asking: why? only because I have been reared in that manner and have had pious fathers for an example. Although I had read all the words of the founder of the testament, I have kneaded the same sourdough which my elders have kneaded in ignorance. I resembled the blind man who sat by the side of the road and heard Jesus, but whose eyes did not behold him. More yet, I resembled the lame man or rather the lazy man, who saw Jesus and heard him, but who was too phlegmatic to follow him, to rise from his berth of habit. Therefore I shall, so I pledged myself in my heart, do honor to God today and, as much as I can, try to do my share to prevent crucification of him who has enlightened me and many other men."

And while I thus spoke and remained alone in my cell, there was a knock upon my door and the Prior of the Benedictines of Augsburg, Xavier Maentlinus, whose brilliant brain you know from Corona, entered and sat down beside me, sighing: "Dear colleague! Augsburg's inhabitants, of worldly and clerical station, have clothed me with the mantle of their trust and have sent me here, to listen to what Hus preaches and what good theories he might have, or advice, to recreate the old apostolic discipline of the church. I'm almost a hundred years old, ninety eight of which I've lived and I do not desire, ere I die, to be buried like a perjurer who speaks differently than his heart dictates. I have come to you to ascertain how you will vote, to-day, ere the day will wane, for or against the life of the Bohemian, because yesterday the youthfully uncouth legate had sworn unchristian like: "And if the Archangel Michael with his hosts, Lucifer with his followers, the German rabble, would hurry to the succor of Hus, they shan't have the satisfaction of liberating the arch-heretic from the purgatory or deliver him from my dagger!" Therefore tell me frankly, how you will cast your final vote. That you might not fear that I will denounce you, I will tell you that I will never vote against him, not even for a penance, because he is Christ's true disciple. My age entitles me to vote first; I shall announce openly before the ears of all hearers that I had been a blind and duped man, whom —the Holy Trinity be praised—God has given a long life, so that he can still behold the rosy dawn of more beautiful and better days of our church and its deliverance from all evil forever!"

HUS THE HERETIC

"My dear, dear Maentlinus!" I cried tearfully, "if all human tortures were in store for me, were I to bear witness for Hus, I would rather bear them than agree with Hus' enemies if even in one point. For he is the star which surely leads to Bethlehem! a cock-crow for our ear, which must awaken everyone who means well, and which must make us sorry for our denial of the Lord, as once had been Peter."

After this and other conversations we walked toward the cathedral, where many curious folk were about and great crowding was evident, so that we had to fight for every step. As yet I had not lost my hope for Hus, because many of the German fathers had spoken in his behalf and without envy. But soon the bells called us again to the church and only through a narrow lane, which the soldiers held open, could we get to our seats. Sigismund, this time, appeared in a Spanish garment of raven-black velvet. A bad sign, I thought! Why coal-black now, when so colorful this morning? Why now a black table and an azure one this morning? Now the chairman rose, bowed deeply and many times to the Emperor and to the assembled fathers. After that he read the name, station, and domicile of each voter, also the names of those who had sent them to Constance, be it a town, a principality, a county or an Imperial Abbey and announced the judges far and wide, after they had answered to the roll call. These were eighty-eight men without the Emperor. There should have been eighty-nine but the Archbishop of Cleve had died at the moment during which Hus truthfully had read his passport. Silently the body had been laid back into his chair, as if he were still alive and had only declined to vote. This happened for this reason: The enemies of the Bohemian were sure to gain their goal on this very day, for the logs for the pyre had already been cut and were drenched with pitch, the work of Ammon Weikhli of Graubuenden, for whom it was a joyous task, to make the arrangements for the spectacle.

The years, moons and days of the voter's ages determined the manner in which the votes were cast, either Yes or No, to three stipulated questions:

1. Shall John Hus of Hussinetz in Bohemia, on account of his reforms and doctrines, be adjudged an heretic?

2. Have the fathers, assembled in council at Constance, in the name of the Holy Father and Emperor, the right and the power to determine the punishment of the church for Hus, and,

3. What punishment shall be meted out to Hus for his blasphemy of the Pope and the holy sacraments?

The first question was answered in the affirmative with fifty-one votes. The second one at once, in the same manner. The third question was answered by thirty votes finding Hus not guilty, eleven votes were for public excommunication, but forty-five votes were for death, should the accused not recant.

Following the polling, the Bohemian was called upon by the chairman to recant everything which he had preached for years against the laws of the church and had taught publicly. But he stood erect and answered for himself in a loud voice: "I can never deny the justification for my teaching and believing in the gospel of Jesus Christ and so God wills, my strength shall remain within me constantly, as long as I have not been proven wrong by the holy bible. Whenever this is done, I shall laud the customs of the church to the full extent of my power." Sigismund several times asked the Bohemian, urgently and well-meaningly, to retract. Whereupon Hus sank upon his knees and prayed loudly and devotedly to God, to enlighten his heart and head and to show him the road to the truth and guide him, should he have erred and strayed from the path. This was his prayer, such as I have never heard in equal devotion, like that of a divine high priest of the old and Jesus of the new belief. But many of the delegates made fun of it and noisily demanded a vote. Even against the Emperor's will they raised a great hubbub and urging, so that the supplicant arose and remained silent to all that which was brought forward against him by the witnesses who had been recalled.

HUS THE HERETIC

Sigismund sighed often, burdened and deeply, his usually sanguine face was deathly pale and his eyes rolled about uneasily, as if he sought something or feared a terrible wrong. But when all had grown peaceably and silent again, Hus spoke once more: "I have bowed before God and prayed for his help in my tribulations, but I have not changed my mind, so that I might recant, if only one sentence, of which I have written and claimed. But that I know and will guard against, that all witnesses have borne false witness against me in what they have said and insisted upon. Their oaths are but black pitfalls, for they are far removed from the truth, such as God knows. At any rate, I find solace with the other heralds of the truth who have been brought from life to death by false witnesses, not because they have stated simple opinions about the holy sacraments, their use in single or twofold form, nor for the reason that they have preached against the rottenness of the clergy, but because they have spoken or borne witness against the Roman bishop, that he is equal to others in his office; for that reason they were tortured and have been slain. Just as it had been meted out to me by inquisitors and blind maniacs, sent by Rome."

At this, a terrible yell of condemnation arose, and demand for a vote was made, which was taken at once. First the electors or their deputies voted, then the cardinals, the arch-bishops, the bishops, then the deputies of the counties and towns, according to their age. The first vote was cast by the Elector Ludewig of the Palatinate, then the others as follows:

Elector Ludewig: Even if I am opposed to all reforms in matters of the church, do not tolerate them nor further them, I have been aware for too long a time of many facts about the clergy and the discipline of the church in need of censure, that I could conscientiously liken Hus to the devil or condemn him to death. For this reason I am willing to use, whatever good he has taught, in my own lands, with the hope to harvest good grain in coming days. To what extent he might have erred, I believe that penance is sufficient to find therein a punishment; but least of all shall Hus be deprived of freedom, honor or life, because he has come here in all earnest, trusting to an Imperial letter of safe conduct and to German word of honor, and secondly, because he has given straightforward answers to all questions and has offered to recant as soon as he was proven wrong out of the Biblia sacra. The testimony against him he has never regarded seriously, but merely as hired perjury. For this reason I vote, for his liberation and safe return home, with—**Yes**.

Von Einbecken, confessor of the Elector of Saxony, as delegate: Shall I publicly speak as a priest, then I must loudly deplore that it is not at all honorable to see Hus incarcerated by us like a common thief, since he has been ordained and is a servant of the altar, whom it is forbidden to insult. Here at Constance naught was thought about to give a spectacle before all the world, which makes one ashamed. One has seen priests and laymen threaten with murderous weapons, a man commended to protection, a man who voyaged defenselessly into a foreign land, one has cast him into the cell of a murderer without trial and justice and has laughed at his prayer to God for enlightening. Not even a heathen would do that, least of all should a Christian do so to another. That I had never expected and when I return home I must hide my face in shame, while I report to my Prince the final result we have arrived at in our council and what sort of tools we have used in building the divine church. Instead of permitting the herald of new doctrines to speak freely, one has silenced his lips with noise and stamping, so that his purpose would be defeated and the clearness of his argument would not rear its head; all this is the work of a united and evil minded majority. I demand therefore, first of all, further time to decide upon a sentence for Hus and secondly that the Bohemian be discharged and acquitted, because he is not a criminal, but a man of high courage, noble learning and one with royal commendation. Following this, I manfully call attention to the fact that any harm done to one standing under the protection of a foreign power will bring censure, vengeance and more discomfort to the entire clergy than might be foreseen. I vote for freedom, honor and life. **Yes**.

HUS THE HERETIC

Koengel, delegate of the Elector of Mainz: My Prince Prior of Mainz believes a renegade of Rome, whatever his error or mistakes might be, to be a lost sheep, to which one must whistle and call lovingly and kindly, until it returns to the fold. If it does not hear, then it is to be urged to return, first with pebbles and then with hard clumps of earth. If this method does not bring it back, then the watchdogs have the order to destroy the stubbornness of the erring one in the seed, be it with sharp teeth biting the ear or by choking it by the throat. Hus is erring, for this reason the shepherd at Rome has first called to him, then thrown stones after him and then only had he taken refuge to painful punishment for the sake of the rest of the herd. If he does not recant anything—may he choke!—No.

Eutropius, delegate of the Elector of Trier: It is quite an old wisdom that a mangy sheep will contaminate the whole herd and the wise keeper of a sick animal will segregate it and, when it is incurable, will kill it, so that he will not become a poor man through an evil which he was able to prevent. Hus is a poisonous, mouth diseased beast, for which there is no remedy; for that reason I cannot share the fears of the voter from Mainz and I propose solitary confinement for Hus; should this mild sentence bear no fruit or should, with his knowledge, his friends arise to liberate him, then only shall he be killed. So that his life may be spared now, I vote, in the name of my Lord—**Yes**.

Elector of Cologne: Whosoever does not heed a warning, must heed the whip. And when both do not accomplish a result, as shown by the Bohemian, then he is akin to the unfortunate whom the rope at the gallows must educate.—No.

Richard Rudolf, Governor of Frankonia, delegate for his brother, the Elector of Brandenburg: All the prayers of the priests in the world would not atone for the innocently shed blood of a brother. I take courage to say, after all that I have heard, that Hus is neither a beast nor a mangy sheep, but that he is a good shepherd and many times better than some at Rome. That he truly tends his flock and waters them with clear water, may be seen from the fact that no falling leaf from a tree can frighten, nor that a grim wolf can terrify his herd, but that he seems willing to risk his life for his charges. Far be it therefore from me that I should become a brother of Cain, so that I, if not exactly before the world, but before the remembrance of Abel's death, would become a fugitive until the end of my time. I vote for freedom and life.—**Yes.**

Count Chlum, in the name of the Elector of Bohemia and his King Wenceslaus: It is for the first time to-day that I fight with my tongue, like papists and women, instead of with my sword like a warrior and that I change such a dire misfortune into an accomplishment. When six years ago the Primate upon the chair of Peter at Rome made war upon the King of Hungary and sent messengers to Bohemia for help, it would have been within our power and even to our gain, to draw our swords in the support of the heir to the Hungarian crown, and more so, because the right was on his side in his argument with Rome. But we decided to bring about peace between the two, conflicting factions, which object we achieved, with the help of much gold, to the advantage of our highest bishop. For a full year Rome ladled out to us promises and counter offers of love, until in our lands an evangelical-apostolical spirit, sponsored by John Misnensis, John Hus, Anthony Zertsch and Jerome, then living in Prague, became rife, to which thousands and more thousands of hearts turned, because the whole clergy had become but a despised crowd of fornicators and ignorants, who had made their belly their God and who loved a godly life less than swine love a mirror. For a long time we had protested against such conditions to the chief shepherd, but instead of a change for betterment, it now has become still worse and the rules and the fees for the indulgences have increased. Again, due to an unjust war against the King of Naples, the Roman ruler of Peter's see sent a sizable army of begging monks into all Christian lands, including Bohemia, with these rights and powers: to forgive to all those, who would serve him against his enemy, be it with their money, possessions or blood, their past and future sins for all times. For this reason unrest started among the thinking people, the indulgences were burnt and the begging monks, who overran the land, were chased away. This caused a great deal of crying and wailing among the papists, as if injustice had been their lot, and it seemed as if it would be necessary for those who had refused to submit, to seek forgiveness upon the knees. Zertsch, the gray-haired priest of Wrallasch was cited to Rome and he made a pilgrimage there, trusting in the righteousness of his complaints, but he never returned home. He has vanished from the ranks of the living. Three others, of the same opinions, were decapitated by the command of arch-bishop Sbynko, their torsos were burnt and their ashes cast out from the grace of the church. Thousands received humiliating penalties, an unseeming end was meted out to them, they were deprived of heaven's joys and a never ending hell fire was prepared for them on earth. Against these acts Hus raised his voice and he was ordered to Rome. He did not dare to undertake the journey, for just reasons, so he was induced to come to Constance to talk freely before the fathers of the church. Immediately after his arrival he was cast into prison, despite of an Imperial letter and promise of safety. Advocate and defense were denied him and he was tortured with questions. Due to the presence of witnesses unknown to us, the hearing became in inquest, the opinions became condemnations to-day, the end of a mock-trial, which threatens the life of the enlightened man, to the shame and eternal dishonor of every German and the whole clergy. But I promise this to you and take an oath, in the name of my King and all Bohemians: If Hus will be tortured any longer and should he pay with his life, the men of Bohemia will make a terrible vengeance upon churches, monasteries and lewd papists and a thousandfold they shall repay just as his enemies deserve it. Peace has been disturbed before God and men and the Bohemian goose shall cleanse her feathers in the blood of Roman adherents. Whosoever has ears to listen, listen then! Life and freedom for Hus!—**Yes.**

Archbishop Namegi: Life and freedom I wish and hope for all men, especially for those who labor to free souls from sin and evil and that minds turn more to God. That Hus has both final goals in mind is recognizable and has been proven right by his doctrine and his exemplary life. Even if he could have lifted the roof of the sinful house a little more carefully, in doing so, not he has committed an act punishable by death, but those who have blinded the window of light and have entombed it. Hus shall live! Indeed—**Yes**.

Archbishop Celc (from Hungary): Whosoever seeks angels upon earth, may be sent to heaven! Hus seeks angels, for this reason may he receive the favor to be sent where he may find them.—May he die—to-day!

Archbishop Styrum (from Vienna): It seems to me, that all about us is night, in which we snore; would it not meet with everyone's approval, had they the wisdom, if some of us would wake while other sleep, like the disciples at Gethsemane? Would not our council be like the foolish virgins who emptied their oil and, waking, extinguished their lamps, if we would extinguish such watch-torches like Hus? Not such be our lot! Whether or not Hus has practiced heresy has not been proven and even if he would bear such a disease upon his body, may the doctors learn from his illness how to cure him.—**Yes**!

Archbishop of Rheims: If God looks in favor upon a new belief, let him work a miracle now; if not, may the Bohemian comet perish.—I vote for death!

Archbishop of London: And if the Bohemian long neck had ten lives, I would take seven of them for his talk against the holy sacraments, firstly because he has blasphemed the master upon Peter's chair, and then because he disrobed the clergy and has not left them even as much as a shred to cover their nakedness; thirdly, because he has misled many ignorant people, who cannot draw a just conclusion and who are better off if they do not see the light and retain a simple faith. May the Bohemian die!

Bishop of Bamberg: Before the storm rises and the waves rock the vessel, a cautious pilot tries to furl his sails and coil his ropes, because it is to his advantage to do so when adverse currents begin to set in and danger threateningly embraces him. Just so precaution forces us, who stand at the wheel, to part the swirling, restless waters, so that we may not be engulfed, which can be accomplished only by breaking the tumultuous whirlpool, created by Hus and his companions to trap the ship of Peter. For this reason it is better that one or several die before the whole crew perishes. May he drown in the depth which he has changed into a whirlpool. Neither freedom nor excommunication. I vote for death!

Bishop of Brixen: It is nothing for a goose to be cleaned and roasted. We have started to clean her, let her be roasted—to-day!

Bishop of Basle: An eye for an eye, a tooth for a tooth, Hus shall roast!

Bishop of Chur: I vote for freedom, honor and life! Because it is true that, if you will roast the goose, a mighty storm will carry her feathers all over the lands and they will be gathered up eagerly, here, there and everywhere. Up to now, the finders have dipped them only into black ink, to write articles in defense of Hus. But if you will spill the blood of the goose, her quills will be dipped into blood and will write redder than the fiery shafts of lightening, so that the writing will be visible, even to the unseeing eye, in brilliant letters in the blackest night. For this reason and many other considerations, I counsel Christian mercy, because the experience of every one of us must and will say that all too hasty acts will bring more disaster than favors. The stone, which we are about to throw towards the clouds might easily fall upon our heads.

Bishop of Eichstaedt: In casting our votes to-day we must consider the past, the present and the future. If we ask ourselves, what have the bloody verdicts, from the beginning of the power of the church, accomplished against heretics, renegades and heathens? Nothing! Of those, to this day, there are still great numbers. But the mild understanding of Wahnfried, Christostomus and Steven have turned more souls toward Rome than all the sword carriers and spearmen of the mighty. If we will take the example of the past to teach us the present, the answer will be: use clemency at all times! Regarding the attention the doctrine of Hus demands now, I am of the opinion that we should first examine the defects and the brittleness of the cloth of the church, and if it is found that such defects adhere to it, as we have been told, then it would be wise to purchase a new garb, in which the clergy might walk about in honor and not like the foolish, who cover the rents in the defective coat with new patches and labor on a useless piece of work which will necessitate a new habit in a few moons, at any rate a garb which will keep out the storm and the wind in future. In such an unwise manner we have looked upon the past, present and future and for this reason I shall by no means vote for Hus' death, but for his protection at all time, as a German word of honor demands.

Bishop of Freising: We shall not believe ourselves to be masters and preceptors in matters pertaining to God, nor believe this of anyone, just to please Him, but we shall place ourselves under the mastery of Christ and his teachings and primarily ask him for guidance and enlightening. Item: I do not claim to be a rabbi. I am only a poor pupil before the Lord, who is aware only too well of his weakness, ignorance and sins. How could I therefore be foolish enough to treat my neighbor other than I am. For this reason honor and freedom for John in the desert!

Bishop of Fulda: We must be very careful not to permit rebellious people, who lean toward Hus, to gain the upper hand. Not because we would have to fear a loss upon our own body, but because it is known to everyone, that sects, even if there should be a lot of good in them, are quite often proud, stubborn and difficult people, who ask of others tolerance, but do not practice it themselves. With this the predicants are not satisfied. My counsel would be to place adequate quarters at the disposal of the Bohemian where he might find time to ponder about his doctrine. In addition to this he shall submit his case in writing, but in such a manner that his writings might be looked into by his superiors and the good points, as far as such are contained, might be converted to the benefit of all Christians, as has been done by the imprisoned John upon the island of Patmos. In this manner, many people who follow Hus, would not be incited, a mighty King would not be insulted, the Emperor's letter of guarantee of safe conduct would not be ravaged, German honor would be saved, the Pope glorified and the clergy cleared from a debt of blood. Without clemency there cannot be a united church in the future, especially not if we become bloody judges, from which God may preserve us. I vote therefore for banishment into a Bohemian cloister!

Bishop of Hildesheim: There is no man who cannot be replaced if he should die, for this reason no one's death is an irreplaceable loss for the world. But the life of a single person may become dangerous to the institutions of the world and in such a case his sacrifice is a benefit to society. That such a sacrifice should be made by Hus is my conviction and I vote for—death!

Bishop of Osnabrueck: Uncounted numbers have died for our belief. First let Hus, and many of his followers, die for the sake of his doctrine, then we shall congregate again and counsel what shall be done. May he die in the fire!

Bishop of Paderborn: Moses preached the hope, Christ the belief and the Pope obedience. The Bohemian does not want to obey, for this reason may he die!

Bishop of Liege: Whosoever reaches for the crown of the Pope or the belly of a papist, is a bold jester; but whosoever teaches the bible to the common rabble, casts pearls before swine and thus sins against the holy ghost. For this reason I condemn Hus, since he does not reclaim his pearls, to the stake!

Bishop of Passau: "He who blows out a light, loves primarily night and sleep. I take Hus for a light, which well graces the long winter night of our church. I think that such a bright flame should not be forcefully extinguished, more so, because there is too much sleeping done by young and old. I vote for honor and life and freedom.—**Yes**.

Bishop of Salzburg: There is something not clear to me, something distrustful about our verdict of to-day, and our speeches have little of the apostolic spirit, as long as we do not shed the old garment and don the new, since, honestly spoken, it was only a cover for lies and not the truth, such as everybody should have for his neighbor; because we are all brothers in Christ. For this reason I shall not condemn my brother, because who among us is a just man? The Lord does not love those who walk in pride before him; for those of righteous heart he builds a temple. Honor, freedom and life to the accused at all times.

Bishop of Speyer: A council of the fathers of the church ranks higher than the life of the pontifex at Rome, let alone, the life of a disobedient priest. But since it is not a fault in my eyes if a man obeys God and his conscience more than man, I do call Hus' fortitude an accomplishment and I do by no means wish to soil the same with the manure flowing from the stinking glands of persecution of others. I vote for life and freedom. **Yes**.

Bishop of Constance: Six times the sun has labored through her circle since the last heretic was burned upon the town common of Constance. If Hus will not be roasted here to-morrow, then the people will roast all of us to-morrow, all those who convene here. May he die!

Clemens Rohan, coadjutor of the bishop of Strassburg: All the waters of the Rhine could not wash the odium of shedding Hus' blood from our clergy and the waters would carry the shame of such an injustice even to foreign lands beyond the sea. What good would our grandchildren inherit from us, if we besmirch the trust of one, founded upon our protection? The accused shall go in peace, for he obeys God more than man!

HUS THE HERETIC

Bishop of Trient: And if the Bohemian were my grandfather, I should cause him to roast!

Abbot of Stablo and Malmedy: A small bird may cause an avalanche by alighting upon a snow-pregnant branch, growing on the side of a steep mountain, an avalanche which might bury thousands and cause dire misfortune. The tongues of Hus and his companions have wagged enough and his helper's helpers have pushed the slaughter-block far enough into the land, so that, if we do not overwhelm them soon, they will cast us upon it and kill us, with much ado and much derision. For this reason I vote for death.

Delegate Mergentheim of the Austrian Order of the High and German Masters: Half measures are void and the hours of the church's opportunity are waning quickly! May he die!

Delegate of the Grandmaster of Malta: Rome's messengers of salvation have not waded through swamps, crossed the seas, wandered through deserts, scaled mountains, tamed wild hordes and fought wild beasts to spread the gospel of Christ and fortify the power of Peter's chair, so that a vain monklet from a dark land of barbarians might speak in derision of all those labors and endeavor to raze the house built during many centuries of toil and to grind the rock, upon which it rests, to dust; no, thus be not the fate of the mother at whose breasts thousands have happily rested and were suckled. Hus shall burn and die!

Knighted Abbot of Corvey: Never have I been so sick of life than now, while I have been sitting in judgment at Constance. I was young once and have now grown old, much have I seen and heard, I also wallowed often in the sensual mire of fornication, have consorted with many of impure heart in my young years, but never have I encountered such iniquity as that which is being committed here upon a just man. I am asking, first of all, who among you has disproved but one point of Hus' theories? You cannot earn much glory by cursing like warlike folk and by showing your teeth like wolves to a hunted doe. It is really lie and deception what the Bohemian's tongue is saying, especially of the sacraments, the infallibility of the Primate at Rome, the abuse of the confession, the obedience and the peddling of indulgences? Item: Has your cry of damnation against Hus made fertile the desert of the clergy and changed it into gardenland? Is not the lament of Crispin, who is honored as a Saint, that of Hus, which he sings before all people: "The life of the lights of the church is a den of iniquities where even the truth is being questioned!" I have seen upon my journeys how those, who preach from the pulpit, live contrary to God's commandments, contrary to order, law and human usage, feast and drink, hold orgies and think as little of the scriptures as a donkey does who passes a hitching post. In their intercourse with gentlemen they are hypocrites, flatterers and two-faced clowns; instead of to punish the sins of the gentry, they are afraid of them and crawl like dogs before them. Turning away from God, they know nothing but to rob offertory and sleep in peace, which they consider a good day's work. They keep their mouths shut; if they open them, they bark at poor souls who never have had a good time in all their lives and whose days end under the burden of severe penalties. They gently question great rulers, counselors, noblemen and gentlemen about their misdeeds and alot easy penance, forgive their sins, sing the litany at their graves like perjured hirelings, laud their stinking paths of life, as if they had done nothing else but skin an orange or a pomegranate. This has been my own experience and just because Hus censures such a manner of living and exposes it, he is to be punished? How can you justify such conduct before God and the world? Never! As long as there is a watchful conscience in my heart and that of all men, I cannot believe, nor permit that we do such an injustice to this truly honorable Bohemian. I vote for honor and life!

Knighted Abbot of Kempten: The sword in my hand against all the world means more to me than the key of the church at the bottom of the Tiber! Death to every heretic, especially to the Bohemian one!

HUS THE HERETIC

Prior of Ellwangen: I'm not at all an orthodox voter and always love light and truth; but I am not so sure that such seeds as Hus is planting will not bear poisonous fruit, as was proved in the past. That we are called upon to destroy weeds, cannot be doubted. We have tended the tree, waited to see if it would bear pleasant fruit and our hope has been blighted. We have granted it another year and again the crop showed tainted fruit; for this reason it should be cut down and cast into the fire, if possible, today!"

Maentlinus, delegate of Augsburg: When I heard the doctrines of Hus, I said, just like Zacharias in the temple: "Oh Lord grant thy servant to depart in peace, for now mine eyes have beheld the saviour of the church." To my sorrow I admit that many of the fathers, here assembled, do not share my joy, but find it condemnatory. Even if I should endanger my ninety-eight years, end my earthly career by fire and sword, I shall not place a lock upon my lips, so that it cannot be said of me, later on: Augsburg's voter has had part in Hus' blameless death, by casting a negative vote. I am sitting here as the oldest and my long life has led me through much sorrow, but the heaviest sorrows were those which the laws of the church have brought me. My father was a dealer in garnets, diligent, honest and frugal, true to his faith, although many doubting opinions could be heard in the city of my birth. My mother is said to have been a beautiful maiden, barely nineteen years of age when my father married her. Together they saved a considerable fortune, which they increased by peaceful diligence and frugality. It so happened that my grandmother laid down to die and she confided in the priest, who heard her confession, that she might die contented and at peace with the Lord, were it not that she had broken a vow at the time when Agne, my mother, had been married, since she had promised the child, while she was still carrying it under her heart, to the church. The father-confessor wrote this confession down and caused it to be signed by witnesses. As soon as my grandmother had died, the church claimed my mother and all her possessions. My father refused to obey, because he loved his wife more than his life, for she was beautiful, virtuous and had borne him a boy, myself. For three years my father fought the church for his right; then he received at Rome, to where he had pilgrimaged, the final verdict, according to which he was declared to be wrong, that the convent could rightly claim my mother and all her possessions. My father was excommunicated, because he was stubborn, my mother was brutally torn from him, and by verdicts rendered simultaneously at home, at Rome, at Vienna and by Emperor Louis, the fifth of his line, he was deprived of all his earthly goods. Deserted by his friends, for he had been cast out of the church, he hung himself at the gate of the Ursuline Convent, behind which he believed my mother to be incarcerated. His body was publicly burned, to which spectacle I was led, a five year old boy, by the same father-confessor who was the cause of it all. I never saw my mother again and the poorhouse and the parish school became my lot, where I had to fast and suffer. While the prior and the monks swallowed delicious viands, I had to wait at the table, naked on warm days and only partly clothed on colder days and quite often I had to stand before them in my nakedness, so that they might enjoy the sight. A flood of wine came from Suabia, as it is even today, and the money to pay for it was taken from the church collections and the estates left to the church. Whenever priests visited and were full of the wine, the secrecy of the confession was violated and in lascivious words they recounted, how their flesh had sinned against the holy ghost.

With such an example I did not grow up as a well behaved child should and I did whatever my heart desired. Although I was a priest, under the oath of chastity, I kept concubines without shame and fear, because others even outdid me in this and nobody had courage enough to clean out the dung heap. Such was my life until I was forty years old. The dispensation of the Elector of Bavaria furnished the reason for a journey to Rome. Full of contrition I fell upon my knees and prayed to God and the Holy Virgin to forgive me my sins and piously I wandered toward my goal, which I imagined to be a sanctum and a divine Jerusalem, where those of unclean heart were punished on soul and body. But how disappointed were my hopes! Babylon could not have been vainer, Sodom not more lustful and Jerusalem, the beautiful, not more proudful than Rome. Item: All the brilliant majesty of Solomon's court was darkened by the splendor of Peter's chair, upon which Benedict sat, at that time. Everything which is registered in the book of the world's sins and iniquities was committed by all those who either wore the purple or the monk's habit, just as they still do, to-day. My sins shrank to insignificance before those which I witnessed in Rome. I was kept there in comfort and noble surroundings for thirty days, after I had turned over half a ton of gold to the Holy Father. Fed up with the sight of such sinning, I turned my feet homeward. Fifty years have passed since that time and more and more the clergy turns to evil, so that Rome's cup of sin overflows, to the consternation of all those who are of pure thought. Therefore listen to the voice of Hus in the wilderness, so that the Lord's eye shall not seek a just man in vain and fire shall not drop from heaven to exterminate us all. Give heed to the voice of your conscience, listen to the truth and honor the Lord, the Virgin and all Saints by honoring the Bohemian. Listen to his words and ascend out of the destruction, before the waters of retribution rise above your heads. Honor, freedom and life to the accused! **Yes**!

After Augsburg's voter in favor of Hus' life, there followed twenty-one votes for death, cast mostly by delegates from Switzerland, France, Italy and England, until my name was called. This I said, my dear Nikolai: "Mine has been a great misfortune, venerable fathers, in that I had to be the messenger to Hus, whom at first in my blindness I believed to be dangerous and whom I sorely persecuted; but since I have heard his voice, recognized the truth of his words, heard of his sorrows and brought them to light, his fortitude under punishment and incarceration has gained a place in my heart for him and I pity him that he should have been lured here and robbed of his freedom and was prosecuted for spreading the gospel of Christ. In all that he has said so far and in all his answers to the questions put to him, I have not been able to find one misstep, for this reason I wash my hands of the blood of this just man, should you spill it for the sake of your earthly gains and because you do not wish that the iniquity of the clergy be exposed to all the world. How long does earthly happiness last? Only a little while! But a good name lasts into eternity and such I wish to preserve for my people, of whom I'm one. I vote for freedom, honor and life — **Yes**!

Vincent Ferrerius was the last one of the Latins who spoke for the rescue of the noble Bohemian, although he had been the former confessor of Pope Benedict. He said without hesitating: "Even if this priest from the Bohemian lands, whom love for truth, confidence in the word of man and thirst for wisdom have led to Constance, into the council of men of his station, had come to spread the gospel of Lucifer, the chief devil, I would not tolerate that he be betrayed, because a betrayal is worse than all sins taken together. How much more must I protect him, since God's word testified for him. Who among us is not ashamed of youthful sins? Hardly a one! And only he would be like Hus, who has walked the straight path in the sight of all men, and none of us are entitled to cast a stone at him. For many weeks I have been sitting here, but out of the many idle talk and balderdash I have not heard one accusation against Hus, which he has not been able to contradict conclusively. No accusation had been weighty enough to rightfully imprison him, and to let him end at the stake, dishonorable and shamefully! All your behavior and your dealings with this rare man urge me only to spit in disgust and to call: thrice shame! If such misdemeanor is meted out to the sapling, what will you do the dry branches? Verily, you are blinder than a blindborn and more stubborn than the heathen, if you believe that by roasting the tongue of this John the Baptist you will sear the fresh greening of his teachings! Not so, I tell you. Even if the greening corn had been scorched by your fire, the stones would cry out and if the stones had been melted by the heat of your fire, they would change into glass and recreate, in thousand colors, the torch of Truth called Hus. Or do you believe that you can destroy the soul with the body? If so, you sit in sorrowful darkness! Your intelligence would have to envy the beasts of the forest, the vermin which creeps in the dust at your feet and you would have no hope for salvation if your dirty house of cards would fall down and be pissed upon by prowling dogs. No, no! you must always believe, if you care to or not, in a retribution beyond and even if you do not practice what you preach to the common people, you will never find solace in life and a heaven after death! Therefore be lenient with your enemies. Jesus said: "Blessed are those who are of clean heart; for they will see the Lord!" but if you will become murderers of your brother, how will you be able to further pray to God at the altar or in your cell: "Forgive us our trespasses as we forgive those who trespass against us!" Would you not, so you condemn Hus, condemn yourself before Him, who sounds hearts and who is a just judge; would you not condemn yourself when saying the Lord's prayer, if you still say it? You would frivolously throw away the consolation of the forgiveness of sins and end your days, sooner or later, like those who have no hope! And finally, do you not fear the vengeance of those who follow Hus, if you insist on torturing him much longer and finally will kill him? I say to you, streams of innocent blood will be spilled for his sake, because you love sin and iniquity more than truth, justice, peace and virtue. Woe to the Pope, woe to all of you who seek the rock of Peter with such stinking laughter! In the name of all that is holy, just and honorable, I demand freedom, honor and life for the accused. **Yes**, and yes once more!

Ferrerius' vote only created more bad blood against the accused, because all those who were called upon to vote after him spoke icily for Hus' death. And when the votes had been counted, the number of those who had voted for his death was forty five, without the Roman legate and the Emperor, who, when he had heard the final result, grew deathly pale and trembled in fear, as if he had to pronounce his own death-sentence, although he knew that Hus' liberty and life depended upon him.

The papal cardinal legate did not cast his vote, because enough kindling wood had been gathered without his help.

A terrible silence hung over the entire church after the last speech had been made and then the chairman asked this question of Sigismund: "Mighty Emperor! What does your heart think of Hus' doctrine? Do you believe him to be an heretic who deserves death? Do you wish to pardon him or not?" To which he answered tremblingly: "I do believe that Hus is an heretic and that he, if he does not recant, deserves death at the stake and that I, bound by the oath of my office, cannot save him from the fire. I have in mind to severely censure his adherents in my lands." After he had thus spoken, he arose and wanted to leave. Perspiration stood in large drops upon his forehead. But the papal legate Michael de Causis approached him and asked Sigismund to wait a little while until the sentence was written down and made ready for the signature of his glorious, imperial name. In the meantime Hus, whom the sentence had visibly affected in body and soul also rose and took a step toward the Emperor, calling loudly: "Mighty Emperor Sigismund! How can you dishonor your crown and German nobility by disregarding the letter of safety which you have sent me with your seal and by burdening your anointed head with the curse of infidelity? I do not care about my life, but I am concerned about the loss of your reputation and true majesty, which you will bury alive if you desire my death out of anxious fear to please my godless judges!" Against this Sigismund defended himself: "I have assured you, heretic, only safe conduct to Constance, and such has been your lot. I have neither promised a safe return, nor have I been asked for it. Where then is the reason for your complaint against me? Your superiors have condemned you by a majority." Hus' courage visibly sank. Count Chlum gave him solace and strength with pious words. And when de Causis submitted the bloody sentence to the Emperor for his signature, the Count called to the Emperor: "Caesar, desist from such doings: You are dishonoring your people's name and you are besmirching a countless army of Christian hearts! Desist, desist, I pray in the name of the Holy Trinity! Caesar, Caesar, do not write your name with blood!" But the Emperor's ears were deaf and were further closed by the cardinals, bishops and priests who crowded about him, kissed the hem of his garments and praised his name, when he seized the quill and wrote his name. After the Emperor had risen, the scribe, a monk named Casprici, took the document, lifted it high and read it in a loud voice: "Upon the demand of the mighty Emperor Sigismund and with the holy grace of Pope John, the twenty-third of his line, a council of church fathers was called to sit at Constance, on the shores of the Swiss Lake, to examine the doctrines of a Bohemian called John of Hussinecz, all of which have been found to be teachings of the devil and arch-heresy. The fathers in council have mildly pointed out his error to the Bohemian priest, have shown him the ugliness of his work and have called on him several times to recant his heresy. They have given Hus one year's time to reconsider and since he did not recant, the above named priest has been found to be a stubborn arch-heretic by the majority of the fathers. He was found guilty of being a loose blasphemer of the seven sacraments of salvation of the holy Roman-Catholic Church and is sentenced to be burned at the stake, should he still refuse to recant, which sentence has been voted for by forty-five fathers, been adjudged lawful by the Cardinal legate and has been approved by Emperor Sigismund in his own handwriting in the fifth year of his reign and the fourteen hundred fifteenth of the Christian era. Amen. Constance, the fifth of July."

After the reading there arose a loud controversy about God's judgment upon the others, those of Hus' enemies. The Bishop of London was the one who spoke most derogatory. He whined to Sigismund: "Oh Emperor, you have earned praise out of the mouths of sucklings and little children. You shall be praised eternally, because you exterminate enemies of the true faith and kill their seeds. All past and future sins shall be forgiven you, all misdeeds and errors, whatever they might be. Your name be praised everywhere!" Into this, many voices cried against the papists: "Hypocrites, bloodhounds, slimy creatures are ye, who misuse the name of God to wallow in stinking mire!" Chair backs were broken and the pieces were thrown about. During the tumult the Emperor slid away and Hus could have done likewise without danger; but he still could not believe in his death, trusted in God and went voluntarily to his prison without rancor. The corpse of the prince bishop of Cleve, who had died during the council, was thrown over and trampled beyond recognition, while the mob dispersed. After all this had happened and nobody had remained in the church, Hus was being missed, to the consternation of his enemies. They raised a great noise and hurried to the gates to cut him off, while the bells were being tolled. When they returned from their search, they found him upon his knees in his room, praying devoutly for courage and fortitude. They did not lock his door, but honored the nobility of his soul.

After Hus had finished his prayer, he wrote the following **farewell letter to his friends in Bohemia**: "Dear beloved: The few minutes of life which are left to me, I shall dutifully use to bid you good-bye, for I cannot do more! Fifteen months ago I have left you to defend what I have taught you, before the assembled fathers of the council at Constance. Alas, I have failed in my endeavor, because I was not permitted to speak freely and all my reasons and proofs have been yelled down by grim adversaries from foreign lands, of Latin and German tongues. Two days I had been here, when the order came, for me to appear before the assembled cardinals and to answer to their interrogations. Without misgivings I obeyed the summons. At first their mien was friendly and they were satisfied with the manner and gist of my answers, until their craving for knowledge was exhausted. After that they mildly reproved my cause, warned me formally not to preach any longer the new doctrines, because the common people were well off under the present circumstances and that those who had been schooled in the faith, were to live without taking exception to the clergy, for whom a more cleaner living was to be prescribed in the next edict. Would I consent to let everything be as it was? I would then receive what my heart desired and while they would honor and acknowledge my wisdom, they would guard against my teaching for reasons which they had already mentioned.

Because I did not care to sacrifice my conscience to the fine tongues of these cardinals, they changed their manner. They threatened me with prison, hunger and thirst, which threats they very soon carried out, because I was not permitted to return to my shelter, but was led to a prison cell, far from the center of the town, upon a high wall, where I was locked in and where a soldier stood guard for twelve days. After that I was questioned again and told that a recanting would bring me freedom. But I could not recant without feeling guilty and the promised riches could not change my conviction. For this, despite loud protests against the force and arbitrary will used against me, I was cast into a damp hole in the tower, without hearing, for eighty days. My fare was a porridge, think and salty, my drink was scant water and the light of the day was darkened for me. After that I was asked again whether I had re-considered and my adversaries fawningly tried to induce me to recant before all people. I was ashamed of such doings, because they were against God's word and my conscience and still are.

Then I was cast into a still more dismal prison, where the waves of the lake splashed through the air hole of my cell in the tower and wetted the straw of my bed, so that it became foul and rotted under my body. I had to relieve my bowels into a hole at my feet and often weeks passed before the high waters washed the excrements away, so that a terrible odor remained which nearly killed me. Fever ravaged my bones, a biting rash covered my skin and stinging blisters grew upon my tongue, aggravated by the salty food I received, making swallowing a pain. My teeth loosened and dropped out into the foul straw, my strength left me and the light of my eyes waned. The nails of my fingers grew inward, because I could no longer bite them off and my beard was full of vermin which tortured me continually, bored under my skin and multiplied in the festering sores of my body. My garments rotted and failed to cover my nakedness during the six moons of such imprisonment.

Then I was hauled up again and asked to recant before friend and foe and I — oh how gladly would I keep silent about this — almost losing my fortitude through the suffering I had undergone — recanted what I had taught you, beloved and devoted friends, before those who urged me, and thus earned for myself a better cell. But when I laid down to sleep, the fear for my soul, and remorse gripped me, because I had been illoyal to God and my conscience; I believed to have estranged the angel of God, until I would return again to my faith and in the holy ghost and His gospel.

With the first light of day I informed my enemies that I rued my recanting and with gnashing of teeth and vengeful oaths I was let down again into my hole, in which I had to suffer until a few weeks ago. An escape had been arranged for me, with the help of some who loved me, but my conscience forbade me to avail myself of their help, although no good could ever have come of my refusal. I have grown so sick and weak in body that the end of my days does not frighten me any longer. The only thing which hurts me is that I cannot see you once more in this world and that I must cease to preach the honor of God and the gospel of His Son. Do not grieve, dear friends. God's providence has willed another road for me and even if it is full of thorns and stones, I still hope that it will lead to a victorious goal, from doubt to faith, from wavering to steadfastness.

It also pains me that the servants of the holy church have sunk so deeply into sinfulness and iniquity that they cannot recognize any longer the blackness of their souls and their wickedness, lack the courage to turn from their evildoing and rather drown in oblivion and darkness than to turn and listen to their reason. I cannot remain mute about this wrong and the sins which the majority of the papists have committed against me, how they have cursed, ridiculed me, how they have borne false witness against the path of my life and how they have willfully misinterpreted what I have said, how they have placed over me a devilish scribe, a monk of Einsiedel, who maliciously reversed everything and committed actual forgery. My body is thin and tired, my skin unclean, my eyes have dimmed, due to the undeserved prison which is unsuitable even for murderers, perjurers and adulterers.

My writings, those in the Bohemian tongue, were burnt, although not a word of them had been understood, yea, their wrath went so far that they destroyed a well in Constance, because I had slaked my thirst there, after a long hearing. I write all this for you, my beloved, so that you may know that God has stood by me powerfully in all my tribulations and has strengthened me, so that I might manfully die tomorrow, and I hope that my work will be sealed with the roasting of my flesh. After I shall have departed, the first flight of my soul will be to you, my beloved. Don't avenge my death upon anyone, because nothing can be done without the will of God. Remain peaceful and without rancor. Let the sword remain in the scabbard, so that you may not perish by the sword, avoid sin and iniquity, this is the first duty of the Christian and be mute if the tongues of untruthful enemies sting.

I commend you, now and for all times, your children, wives and servants, the Bohemian lands, yes, the whole world, to the holy trinity. God's angels may guard you against temptation by my enemies, do not permit the pious trust, which I have taught you, to waver. Even if your prayers to God on my account have been in vain, do not doubt because of this; the day of harvest comes even in rainy days. God may grant a wise heart to my King Wenceslaus, that he may reign in wisdom and be blessed, as long as his days are numbered on earth. God grant a joyous soul to my departed Queen, whose father confessor I was. God also grant long life, serenity and happiness to my protector, the Lord of Prachatitz and a happy hour of death. My blessings are for you, who have meant well and my forgiveness be for those who have hurt me at home and in foreign lands. Pray for me, as I pray for you and the whole world. Let the remembrance of me rest in a pure heart and teach your children what I have taught you: to love your neighbor, to be peaceful and modest and then you will fare well, now and in eternity. Farewell, and do not mourn too much for me, for soon my cup will be full. Count Chlum will recount to you everything, how full of fortitude my last road and how godly my end has been. Amen. I would cry much for you, but a servant of God, whose honor shall be mine, must desert, for Him, and for the sake of Christ, his wife, child, brother, sister, home, possessions and all that is dear to him. And so I shall dry my tears and bow under the hand of the Lord. Amen.

Written at Constance, during my last night, on the 5th day of July 1415, on which day I was just 42 years old.

John of Hussinecz

Quietly Hus lay down to sleep, after he had spoken a pious prayer and had handed the above letter to Count Chlum, his friend. A rumor spread that escape had been offered to the prisoner, but he did not avail himself of the offer, because his conscience spoke against it. The door of his cell had been left open and his friends had carried him forcibly upon their arms as far as the street, but he refused to go further, either because he believed that God's hand would rescue him with honor, or because he feared that through his escape he would harm the holy cause which he served and dishonor his own name, upon which the hope of so many had been founded for months. Be that as it may, on the morning of the sixth Hus rose early and sang several psalms. After that he demanded a little wine and some sweet bread. After that had been given to him, he asked to be left alone, then he fell upon his knees, prayed loudly and sobbingly to God, thanked him for the days of his life, for the joys and trials, from childhood until today.

Then he confessed his sins to God, prayed for blessings for his friends and forgiveness for his enemies, blessed the bread for which he had asked and ate it while he spoke the words of the last supper; the same he did with the wine, before he tasted of it. After all this had happened, he prayed again with much devotion, then he walked about in his cell until his friends came to him to take leave. I too, dear Nikolai, called on him again and found him to be of mild demeanor, at peace with the world.

And when I prayed him not to bear malice against me, because I had been the carrier of the letter which had called him into this chamber of woe, he answered modestly: "May God prevent that I shall harbor malice in my heart against someone, because he had not been a Jonathan for me! Does not God make bad days with the good ones, that man might not look into the future? You have shown me a great deal of love by your vote and your pity, for this reason, my dear Poggius, I owe you thanks for the service which you have rendered to me by obeying the command of the Roman Lord on Peter's chair. It has enabled me to become a witness for the truth before all people, which is the blessing of my soul and will so remain to my last hour, which will come today, through my enemies. Today just forty-two years ago, the pitying one has taken me from the womb of my mother and has guarded me to this day, be he praised, for the gift and the taking of my breath, in all eternity."

Now the chimes called to church, to where Hus was led and to where I, and many others, accompanied him, crying hot tears. Again there was a crowding, especially in the church. The Bishop of London preached a long sermon, his text being Romans, VI, 6 of Aristotle and he harangued the Emperor to burn Hus, the arch-heretic, although it seemed that Sigismund was sorry that he had given his signature, by which he had only consented to Hus' death, should he not recant. The Emperor urged Hus to recant his opinions and errors, which were publicly read to the condemned by a fat-bellied monk. Hus stood on a platform, visible to everybody, in priestly garb. After the monk had finished, the Roman cardinal legate asked the accused again to recant, to which Hus answered manfully and with the high courage of the Apostle: "I stand here under the eye of God, and I can never do what you ask me, were I not to blaspheme Him and prostitute my conscience." After this declaration, his bloody sentence was read again, during which act the Emperor fled, as if he had become a malefactor and as if the birds of heaven were calling vengeance.

Now the archbishop of London and that of Rheims approached Hus and placed into his right hand an empty chalice, with the command to drink from it, according to the custom of the priest during communion. Then said Hus: "This chalice, though without wine, shall be filled with forgiveness before all people! If I lack bread, because of the adversity of my enemies, Lord Jesus Christ, my God, provides manna for me!"

These words created much pity for the pious priest, even by some who were against him. When his archenemies noticed this, they jumped up to him, tore the chalice from his right and trampled it under their feet. They raised their fists against him, cursed him after the manner of soldiers, derided him and expectorated into his face. Meanwhile the Englishman cried out: "Oh cursed Judas, who has left the realms of peace and allies himself with the Jews! See, we take from you this chalice, and deprive you of the grace and salvation of the church! Cursed be the day of your ordination, cursed the hour when your pate was shorn and you were anointed with blessed oil. May you dry up like the felled tree, which remains barren in spite of care and attention. Cursed be the spot upon which you have stood and grown, may your branches burn here and everywhere in the devil's eternal oven, you useless bush of thorns! We cast you out of the priestly brotherhood and hand you over to the hangman, so that he may finish with you, evil creature, akin to the poisonous snake and make harmless your drooling fangs among the living! May the sun sorrow for the day on which it still might be said, that Hus the monster, is crawling on earth!"

Alas, drag my poor carcass to death, so that you cannot sin any longer against an innocent victim!" cried the derided man. "Leave the mercy or punishment of my soul to Him who is a just judge and not like you unfortunate blind ones. My trust is in the almighty God and in my Lord Jesus Christ, who has redeemed me and has called me to preach His gospel to the last breath of life. I fervently hope that he may have mercy upon me and receive me in grace and that he will hand to me the cup of eternal salvation and will never take it from me. I also truly believe that he will hand me this cup to-day, out of which I shall drink bliss and my salvation in eternity. His blessed name be praised by all!"

Great shouting silenced the noble martyr. They tore the priestly garb from his body and ripped it to pieces, which they tied to their clothes as a remembrance of their victory over Hus. After that, they fought and argued among themselves whether they should disfigure his head with shears or razor, until they procured shears and pressed his head downward, cutting a star into his hair, while they were deriding him. This displeased many and caused remonstrating. A majority was glad about it and they raised their weapons against

Hus' protectors. There were only a few Bohemians, whom it had been forbidden to bring weapons into the church and they were searched at the door. The Bohemian Knight von Meneczsch, who had hidden a long dagger in the leg of his boot, was in the midst of the crowd and when he perceived his friend's distress, he drew the dagger and plunged it between the ribs of the man who held Hus' head, so that he dropped without a sound. Immediately Hus' enemies turned upon Meneczsch with their knives and tried to kill him, but he was a courageous man, defended himself well and escaped without a scratch, through a small door in the choir. Hus, however, cried and clasped his hand above his shorn head and prayed God for a blissful end.

When Hus stood thus shorn before his enemies, they ridiculed him, threw clumps of earth, moistened by saliva, at him and found it funny when they hit his face. Despite this derision, the poor man remained without hate and consoled himself with the thought of his redeemer, who had borne in silence the scourge and the fists of his enemies. "Why do you mock me? Your shouting cannot destroy the triumph of my heart! I hear sweet music above the heights of Golgotha and the sounds of a joyful Hallelujah, so that Jerusalem's foolish battle cry cannot hurt me at all!" Such praiseworthy words spoke Hus, while they cast him out, half-naked, from the temple of the Lord. Outside of the church, the bishop of Constance placed a paper cap, upon which three ugly devils had been painted, on his head, saying: "Now we deliver you to the worldly courts and your soul we turn over to the devil and his disciples!"

Hus answered to this terrible curse by folding his hands and by praying: "O Lord, Jesus Christ, into thine hands I deliver my soul, which thou hast redeemed with thy blood. Father in Heaven, do not hold against them the sins which my enemies commit against me, and let mine eyes see them blissfully with thee, when their souls fly to thy throne after an easy death. O Holy Ghost, enlighten their deceived hearts, so that the truth of the holy gospel may open their eyes and its praise be spread everywhere, for ever and ever, Amen." The town soldiers had formed a wide circle in front of the church portal, into which the expulsed man was being led. A small fire was lit and several books by Wycliffe and Hus were cast into it, with a lot of shouting. A red-garbed jester moved the books about with a long poker, while he executed peculiar and comical jumps over the fire, so that his feather-tail caught fire and he ran about, crying, in feigned distress, for water. These shameless doings lasted for an hour, during which Hus was often brushed with this feather-tail, from which water was dripping. The sun was high in the skies and sent down much heat. This made many people thirsty and they drank very much of the wine, which was distributed free. They drank so much that they began to be unsteady on their feet, rioted and sang, without regard for Hus' feelings, like barbarians.

These events put off the last moments of the unhappy priest for several hours. During this time there was a kirmess, everybody feasted with viands and drink and they were all eager for the coming spectacle in the evening, young and old, boys and girls and especially the Latin papists, among whom were several who had never seen the roasting of an heretic before. Meanwhile the wood pile had been decorated with motley hangings, tassels, flags, stars and other tinsel, and many women believed it to be good handiwork to burn pieces of their underwear or clothing with the condemned, to atone for their sins or for the sins of those who roast in the purgatory. "Give me a drink of water," asked Hus of his guard, "so that I might refresh my tongue and not die from thirst, lest your joy, to see me at the stake, might be taken from you. I would regret this for the sake of those who have come here to see me burn and have spent so much money on my account."

Full of pity a soldier offered his filled goblet to Hus, but he did not drink from it and asked for pure water, which was given to him at once. This equanimity and piety shown by Hus impressed the heart of the guard. He rose, approached his sergeant and resigned from the service with these words: "I have fought many a battle in my day and I have seen many a brave man die at Raefels in the Glarner lands, at Buergen, Niedau, Unterfern and in the lands of Appenzell, but my old eyes have never seen such courage and fearlessness in the face of certain death. Therefore I think that this Bohemian is a just man, suffering in innocence and I have no wish to serve masters who persecute the feeble and protect the lewd papists. Take back my spear and my sword, for I shall leave Constance today, before the smoke rises to smother Hus and the fires blaze, which will consume his bones."

And so the hour of five of the afternoon came, when the procession started, with Hus, for the Bruehl gate, where, on the left side, the woodpile had been erected and had been splendidly decorated. Three trumpeters upon black horses rode in advance and their loud trumpeting called together the people from afar and drew everybody from the chambers of the houses to the windowsills.

There were only few streets in Constance through which the procession did not wind its way and its duration was longer than two hours. Many cried, many made fun and many prayed for Hus. He sang the praise of God in Latin songs; called out many times with Job the Visited: "My harp also is turned to mourning and my pipe into the voice of them that weep. Doth not he see my ways and count all my steps? If I have walked with vanity or if my foot hath hastened to deceit; if my step hath turned out of the way and mine heart walked after mine eyes, and if any blot hath cleaved mine hands; if I rejoiced because my wealth was great and because mine hand had gotten much; and my heart hath been secretly enticed, or my mouth hath kissed my hand; this also were an iniquity to be punished by the judge; for I should have denied the God that is above? I would be joyous like a King although I go to my death." Then he sang in verse, with an elated voice, like the psalmist in the thirty-first psalm, reading from a paper in his hands:

"In thee, O Lord, I put my trust,
Bow down thine ear to me."

With such Christian prayers, Hus arrived at the stake, looking at it without fear. He climbed upon it, after two assistants of the hangman had torn his clothes from him and had clad him into a shirt drenched with pitch. At this moment the elector of the Palatinate, Ludewig, rode up and prayed Hus with fervor to recant, so that he might be spared a death in the flames. But Hus replied: "Today you will roast a lean goose, but hundred years from now you will hear a swan sing, whom you will leave unroasted and no trap or net will catch him for you." Full of pity and filled with much admiration, the Prince turned away.

Then the hangmen seized moistened ropes, tied the victims hands and feet backward to the stake, squeezed oil-drenched wool between his limbs and the stake and emptied so much oil over his head that it dripped from his beard and he was heard to pray: "Lord Zebaoth! take this sin from them!" After that the faggots were lighted, at six or more places, but they did not burn, because there was too much wool everywhere. Not a breath of air was stirring and the tied man had to wait in fear of death for half an hour, until the smoke started to envelop him.

An old man, almost eighty years of age, carried a bundle of faggots to the stake, lit them and laid them at poor Hus' feet, saying: That you may depart to hell sooner, I bring this bundle, arch-heretic! Whereupon Hus cried out: "Oh holy simplicity!" A thick, stinking smoke billowed and enveloped the unhappy man in black clouds, out of which he was heard to call three times: "Jesus Christ, thou Son of the living God, have mercy upon me!"

After that he became still, the smoke settled and Hus became again visible to all eyes, but his head had sunk to his chest and he had died before a flame had touched him. Two hours later his body had been cremated, after which the ashes were shoveled together, placed into the skin of a steer and then were cast, with jubilations, into the Rhine.

HUS THE HERETIC

I wanted to acquaint you with this story of a heretic, my dear Nikolai, so that you might know how much fortitude of faith Hus had shown before his enemies and how blissful, in his faith, this pious man's end had been. Verily, I say unto you, he was too just for this world!

The Holy Trinity may guard and keep you. This is the wish of your devoted,

Poggius

Written on the day of Calixtus, in October 1415.